The

WHISPERING

WIDOW

APRIL DRAKE

ISBN 978-1-0980-0748-5 (paperback)
ISBN 978-1-0980-0749-2 (digital)

Christian Faith Publishing, Inc.
832 Park Avenue
Meadville, PA 16335
www.christianfaithpublishing.com

Printed in the United States of America

CHAPTER 1

When the new teacher dropped dead on an ordinary Wednesday afternoon, it came as quite a shock!

Right in the middle of my lesson about the New Deal programs of the Great Depression, there came a piercing scream from the room next door. Now, I was accustomed to the occasional racket heard through the wall; Ms. Taylor, whose room was on the other side of that wall, often got a laugh or a shout out of her students. She was very likeable and a good teacher, and, usually, I wouldn't pay it any mind, but there was something of the hysterical in that scream I'd just heard.

Immediately, I yanked my door open to go next door. But I was stopped short before I could get into Ms. Taylor's room by the hulking figure of my own son. I stepped back an inch and looked up at him.

His expression made my blood run cold.

Kids spilled out into the hall behind him, and his best friend, Mattias, took off in the direction of the office.

"Carter—" I barely got the word out before he cut me off.

"Mom, she's dead," he said, bluntly.

"Dead? What? Who—?" It all came out in a jumble as I pressed past him to get through Ms. Taylor's door.

Sure enough, there was Ms. Taylor, face down on the floor. Well, not completely facedown. Her head was turned to the side, her eyes stared blankly, and her mouth was half open as if she still had something to say.

I couldn't believe the sweet, young woman, who loved poetry and was adored by all her students, was really dead!

For the next several minutes, I think I operated on autopilot. I managed to get the door shut since all of Ms. Taylor's class had already fled her room. They were all mumbling and running into each other, so I herded them into Eli Bloom's room across the hall since Eli was on his conference at the time and his door was open, and it was the nearest empty place to corral sixteen half-hysterical, half in-shock teenagers.

I know I was thanking the good Lord about thirty seconds later when I saw Jess Cartwright, our assistant principal and one of my closest friends, quickly followed by the principal and the campus cop sprinting down the hallway. I was all alone in a sea of distraught teenagers, and I felt like I was drowning.

I began to wonder where Eli was; he was another of my long-time pals, along with Bess Wheeler, Jess's twin sister. I always felt more at ease when Eli was around, and, at the moment, I was feeling pretty distraught myself.

Normally, even in a dire situation, I'm pretty calm and collected, but this was my first sudden death. I've lost loved ones, even my own husband, but enduring a lengthy illness or losing someone in a car accident isn't the same as finding a sweet, nice coworker stone dead fifteen minutes after you'd last talked to her.

The rest of the day unfolded in a sort of semi-ordered chaos. To be perfectly frank, I don't remember most of it.

Sheriff's deputies showed up within ten minutes, along with ambulances, but they were too late to help Ms. Taylor. Eli showed up right after the deputies, and I quickly explained what was going on. He stepped over in my room to keep my own students calm and seated while I stood across the hall in his room with Carter.

The loud speaker came to life announcing a soft lockdown, which essentially means stay in your room with your door shut and don't panic. Technically, I probably should have gone back to my own room, but I didn't want to leave Carter. He may have been a tall, strapping young man, but he was still my son, and I needed to be with him. I told all the kids to sit down, but I stayed at the door looking out the window across the hall.

Ms. Taylor was young and healthy. It was her first year teaching with us, but that was long enough for me to know she liked to eat healthy and exercise, so I couldn't imagine why she would have just dropped dead. It had to be one of those silent things, I told myself, like a heart defect you don't know you have until it's too late.

I continued to watch out the window as paramedics and deputies scurried about. I didn't know what the paramedics had to do; I had checked her pulse myself, there was no pulse, she was dead. But there was still a flurry of people in and out of her room.

Eventually, all of the sheriff's deputies that I knew of, plus one I didn't recognize who must be new, were out in the hall. My brother, the sheriff, wasn't there, though. Last I knew, he was transporting a prisoner earlier in the day, so he must have still been trying to get back from that.

Suddenly, I caught sight of Eli across the hall in my room. He was watching me watching all of the activity in the hall. I gave him a weak smile, and he smiled back. Just seeing him made me feel better. There had been many a time when we were kids that he had taken up for me or had been there for me when I needed him for anything.

When we all went to college, we didn't grow apart, we just grew up. Eli met a girl, and I met John. When Eli and I graduated college, he went off to Dallas for a job, and I came back home, went to work, and married John.

For all the years John was alive and with me, he was wonderful. I loved him so! But then one day, he was driving home from work, and it was raining. He hydroplaned, hit a tree, and died on impact.

Eli had just moved back to town a few months before John died. Eli had never gotten married. I knew that because we were still the best of friends and talked all the time, and he came home on the holidays and any other time that he had the chance. It was nice, though, for all my friends and John to be together, in the same town, where we could all see each other and spend time together.

Now, we were kind of back to our younger years. Eli was there for whatever I might need. I was terribly glad he'd made his way back home when he had because I don't know what I would have done after John had died if I hadn't had Eli to lean on.

I shook my head to clear my thoughts and gave Eli a little wave. The kids were getting restless, and I figured it was best to distract their minds for a bit, so I found Eli's dry erase markers and initiated a huge game of SOS on the white board.

CHAPTER 2

A deputy came to the door some time later and said they were going to start questioning people. We filed out into the hall, and the deputies started making their rounds.

The new guy I didn't recognize came to question me and Carter. We got the customary look when Carter called me mom. You'd think I would be used to it by now; we knew we didn't look alike.

It was no secret that I had adopted Carter when I married his dad when Carter was only four years old. At fifteen, Carter already towered over me; he had recently hit six feet tall, and I was only 5'3". Where I had auburn hair and green eyes, Carter had jet black hair and deep blue eyes. He was every bit his dad. Unfortunately, he'd never had the opportunity to meet Anna, his biological mother, but he was still my son.

Carter politely explained our relation as he always did.

The officer, one Deputy Pitt, who was questioning us, nodded and continued on. "So, Carter, before you went to get your mom, tell me exactly what happened."

"Well, Ms. Taylor was writing on the board when I walked in, then she stepped over to the door as the bell rang. A few kids were trying to dart in so they wouldn't be tardy," Carter explained. You could feel the tension in the hall, and I silently prayed that these kids, all of us really, would find peace in this terrible situation. "It was just like any other day. We hadn't been in class very long. She was talking about the story we read yesterday when she paused to take a sip from her cup and then turned back to write on the board. But she never finished writing. In the middle of writing, she turned around, well, staggered mostly, looking kind of shocked. Then she just dropped."

Deputy Pitt made notes as Carter talked.

"Anything else?" the officer asked, looking up from his notepad.

"No, sir," Carter said.

"And, Ms. Kelley?" he asked, turning to me. "What did you witness?"

"There wasn't much to witness," I said, honestly. "I was teaching in my room when I heard a scream. It scared me, so I came to the door, and Carter was there saying, 'Mom, she's dead.' Sure enough, when I looked in, she wasn't moving. I checked her pulse, and she didn't have one, so I just got the kids across the hall. Almost immediately, the principal and the campus cop showed up."

"Did you notice anything out of the ordinary?" he continued.

Other than the dead body? I thought, barely managing to keep my too-often-sarcastic tongue in check.

"How do you mean?" I asked him for clarification.

"Was there anything missing? Did anything look out of place?"

I thought that was an odd question, and just about that time, I saw someone snapping a picture in Ms. Taylor's room. It caught my attention.

What is going on? I thought. I knew if someone suddenly drops dead, the police are called—that's just procedure and everyday common sense. And I'm sure they'd have to question people, but the whole situation just seemed strange to me. Maybe I was being a little dense at the time, but like I said, it was my first sudden death, so I was at a loss of how these things played out.

"Ms. Kelley?" Pitt asked, calling me to attention, while he shot me an annoyed look.

"No, sir," I said, quickly. "To be honest, I wasn't looking around, but the room seemed the same, so I didn't notice anything out of place besides Ms. Taylor. She was perfectly fine when I talked to her before class."

"You spoke to her?" Pitt perked up a bit. "What did she say?"

"After fifth period, I saw her getting a cup of coffee in the lounge, and she told me she was coming to church tonight," I told him. "Then she went back to her room. I was still in the hall when the tardy bell rang. I saw her smiling at the kids trying to scurry into her room to avoid being tardy. Fifteen minutes later, she was dead."

"So you know her outside of school?" he asked, momentarily looking up from his notes.

"Yes, she attends our church. She moved here this past summer and started coming to our church in September. She's been attending church services there ever since," I explained. I was beginning to feel like a gossip airing Ms. Taylor's info.

The deputy had a few more questions about if she ever attended church with anyone in particular, did we know any of her other friends, acquaintances, or family, had she been upset lately?

Right in mid-question, Carter cut the deputy off.

"Why are you asking us all of this?" he blurted out. "You're acting like she was murdered."

The deputy and I went rigid at the same time. I may not have given birth to Carter, but he sure had inherited my big mouth. I wanted to smack my own forehead, but I didn't want to draw any attention to us. I knew Carter was just being his brutally honest self, often he spoke whatever was on his mind, but Deputy Pitt did not look too happy.

"I'm doing my job, young man," Pitt said, firmly. I doubted he was even ten years older than Carter, he sure did look awful young, but he was going to make sure Carter knew who was in authority here. "All you need worry about is answering my questions honestly."

Carter looked a little sheepish. "Yes, sir," he said, quietly.

My mama bear instinct bristled for about two seconds. But I knew Pitt was just trying to do his job, so I told myself to cool it.

A lifetime later, seemingly, the deputy moved on to someone else, and I helped corral kiddos until it was deemed okay for people to leave.

CHAPTER 3

Our principal, Mr. Scott, called an emergency staff meeting that afternoon. Jess went room to room telling all the teachers not to leave campus until Mr. Scott had given his okay, and that wouldn't happen until we all went to the meeting.

I told Carter to walk down the street to the elementary school to get his little sister. I had just called his grandma, John's mother, to come pick them up over at the elementary school.

"Mom," he protested, "can't I just get your keys and drive myself and Darby home?"

"Carter, your teacher just dropped dead in front of you," I argued. "I don't want you two alone right now. Besides, Eli rode with us this morning, remember? I have to drive us home, and you only have a driver's permit anyway."

"Okay, okay," he conceded.

"Okay?" I asked, shooting him my best "mama look."

"I mean, yes, ma'am," he said with a grin. It pleased my heart to have such a polite son. "I'm going. See you at the house."

I smiled back at him. "There's taco soup in the Crock-Pot. Darby needs to take a bath, then eat. If there's any homework—"

"Mama," Carter said then, cutting me off. He rarely called me mama anymore, and it made me realize just how fast he was growing up. After the stressful day we'd just had, I almost got teary-eyed.

"What?" I asked.

"I got this," he said with a grin.

He kissed me on top of the head, and I had to fight off another wave of nostalgia. It had been a long time since I could do that to him. He'd been eye level with me the summer after his sixth grade year, and he only shot up from there. Here, near the end of his freshman year, he was the tallest kid in his class, and he hadn't stopped growing yet.

I usually wasn't this mushy, but the day had been long and stressful. Then I thought how just last week Ms. Taylor had left a stanza from a poem in my box in the teacher's lounge. She said poetry was her favorite thing in the world; when I mentioned that I liked to read poetry, too, she started leaving a snippet of a poem in my box every once in a while. It was a game. I had to guess which poem it was from, without cheating, no looking up the answer, no Internet. It was fun, and I would miss it. Those thoughts only served to make me even more mushy.

I found my friends, Bess and Eli, near the back of the cafeteria, and I plopped down between them.

Eli, Bess, Jess, and I had all grown up together. Jess was the assistant principal, so he was standing up at the front of the cafeteria talking with Mr. Scott.

"You okay?" Eli whispered to me while Bess texted away on her phone.

"Yeah," I said, offering a small smile. "Thanks for asking."

He nudged my shoulder with his. "What are friends for?"

He was smiling at me, and that eased my nerves a little. Ever since we were little, he always was the one to make me feel better when something bad happened. It never had to be a grand gesture or anything out of the ordinary; a simple smile or a few words from Eli always calmed my nerves.

There was a time or two where Eli risked life and limb for me, quite literally. But just to have him near was always a comfort.

Mr. Scott cleared his throat, suddenly, gaining all of our attention. People quieted and sat down if they weren't already. Jess handed Mr. Scott a microphone from the podium on the stage.

"Okay, people, I'll make this brief," he spoke into the microphone from his position directly in front of the first cafeteria table. "It's been a long, tiring day. But I would like to thank you all for your dedication to our students. You all remained calm and kept the children calm and under control. Thank you, Ms. Kelley, for your prompt action as well in getting the kids out of Ms. Taylor's room and corralled until the authorities arrived."

I blushed and looked down at the table as several heads turned to look at me. I wasn't used to being pointed out by the boss.

"Furthermore, if you are contacted by the media, your only answer is, 'no comment.' If they persist, refer them to the office of the superintendent."

I looked up again and saw people nodding around the room.

"Again, thank you for all you've done here today. We will have extra counselors arriving tomorrow to help deal with any grief or troubles associated with Ms. Taylor's death. She was a sweet, young woman and an awesome teacher. She will be missed. I will notify you all when funeral arrangements have been made."

He reiterated his point about not talking to the media and then dismissed us, advising us to all drive home safely.

Almost without thinking, Eli, Bess, and I walked one after the other back down the hall and straight into Jess's office. He was there within a minute after we arrived, and he closed the door behind him.

"Why do I always feel like I'm in trouble when I come in here?" Eli asked as Jess sat down behind his desk.

"Because you always were," I told him, grinning.

Jess and Bess smiled with me at the thought of Eli as a teenager. He was sweet, but tough. He could get into trouble in nothing flat, only to get out of trouble just as quick. Jess may be the assistant principal, but if you added up all the times Eli had had to visit that particular office when we were in high school, he probably spent more time in the place that Jess had in his three years as assistant principal.

"What'd they tell you?" Bess prodded her brother for info.

"Not much," Jess confessed. "The whole situation is odd, though."

"Of course, it is," Eli piped up. "A presumably healthy woman dropped dead in front of a bunch of stunned teenagers. I'd say that's odd."

Jess shot Eli and exasperated look. "I know that," Jess told him. "I mean—well—Quinn, you heard a scream only to go over and find Ms. Taylor dead. What was your first reaction?"

I was dumbfounded for a moment. "Uh, the kids," I stammered. "I tried to get the kids into Eli's room, make sure they were all okay. I mean, I knew she was dead, so I couldn't do anything for her."

"Okay," Jess said, nodding. "But what was your first reaction to her being dead? What did you think had happened to her?"

I thought about it for a second. "I don't know really. An aneurism or some heart defect, maybe. She was barely thirty. Her birthday was last week. I guess I just thought it was one of those quick, silent things like you hear about on the news."

"Me, too," Jess said, nodding again. "But I don't think the sheriff's deputies think that."

"Why?" Eli asked before Bess or I could form the word.

"I don't know exactly," Jess went on. "But I was in here earlier getting my keys, and I heard one of the deputies on the phone. He told whoever he was talking to that he was sending evidence to the county lab."

"Evidence?" Bess gasped. "About what? The woman dropped dead in front of sixteen teenagers. What do they think happened?"

Jess shrugged. "Like I said, I don't know. But right before he saw me he said, 'It definitely looks suspicious, especially since she called us a few days ago'."

"What?" Bess gasped again.

I sat up straighter in my chair. "She? Ms. Taylor? Did she call the sheriff's office?"

"What was she calling about?" Eli chimed in.

"I don't know," Jess admitted, holding up his hands to stop the flow of questions. "That was all I heard. He saw me and went into Scott's office and shut the door."

We all exchanged curious, confused glances. Then, Jess leaned forward, over his desk, and we all leaned in to hear as he lowered his voice.

"But I don't think they think she just dropped dead," Jess admitted. "I think that they think someone killed her."

CHAPTER 4

I was quite sure Jess wasn't really supposed to be telling any of this to us, but we'd all been best friends since the womb, so we were rarely able to keep things from each other. Jess asked us to keep what he'd just said quiet, and then we filed back out of his office to head home.

Bess had all her things with her, so she said goodbye at the office and left for home. Jess went and made his rounds to make sure all the doors were locked, and Eli walked with me back to my room.

Ms. Taylor's door had been crisscrossed with police tape. I could see Deputy Pitt through the window in the door. He was talking on his cell phone.

Eli saw him, too. "I don't think he knows your brother is the sheriff," he commented.

I shrugged as I unlocked my own door, and we went in.

"So," I said, "what does that matter?"

He sighed. "I just don't think he'd have been so short with you and Carter earlier if he knew."

I remembered Pitt's questioning earlier. He wasn't rude; he just seemed to have wanted to assert his authority with Carter. I just shrugged it off as I grabbed my purse and turned off my computer.

"You know I'm not like that, Eli," I told him as I closed the blinds. "I don't point out that my brother's the sheriff. I don't need any special treatment out of people."

"I didn't really mean it like that," Eli said with an exasperated sigh.

When I turned from the blinds, Eli was standing a few feet away, arms crossed. He didn't look happy.

He actually looked angry, a look I'd grown to know over the years. When we were kids, this look was usually preceded by Eli flying off the handle and slugging somebody. Some of the behavior was in my defense, so I couldn't fault him for it.

Most of the time, he was a sweet, gentle guy, laid back, and easygoing. But, oh boy, watch out if you ever hurt one of his friends! Come to think of it, that was about the only time he got really angry, when he felt someone was hurting his friends.

Right then, he was looking pretty incensed. But Pitt really hadn't been rude, just very straightforward.

"Eli, what's wrong?" I asked, walking over to him and putting one hand on his crossed arms. "I'm fine. Carter's fine. Shocked, yes, but we're okay."

He uncrossed his arms suddenly and let them hang loosely at his sides. He offered me a warm smile, so I smiled back.

Then a thought occurred to me.

"You know, Eli," I said, a little mischievous, "you were acting like this on Saturday when we were at Borden's birthday party at the park. Some guy in the parking lot yelled at me. He said I took his parking spot. Carter and I had to hold you back."

He blushed suddenly and looked away. "Yeah, sorry," he said, then tried to laugh it off.

I grinned a little more, too, and wrapped him in a hug. Eli, Bess, Jess, and I were inseparable, and Eli never failed to take care of me when I needed it. I enjoyed having Eli's strong arms around me—it was comforting, and I felt safe.

"I lose my head sometimes when I think somebody's treating you wrong," he said giving me an extra squeeze, then pulling back to look at me.

I had to look up at him; we were standing so close. His hands still rested on my waist, and mine were still on his shoulders. We must have looked like two people preparing to slow dance, but never moving.

"I'm not complaining," I told him, still smiling. "I just... noticed, that's all."

We stared at each other for a few more moments. We had been friends since before we were old enough to remember anything. But lately...

But lately, nothing. For a while now, I'd begun to notice what I could only assume others already saw every day. Eli was a tall, handsome, strapping man. Tan skin, coal black hair, beautiful dark eyes. But it wasn't just that. I already knew the most important parts about him—he was a Christian, he cared deeply for me, he was kind, and he's already stuck by me through every tragedy I'd faced in life.

We jerked apart suddenly as someone cleared their throat.

"Sorry, folks." It was Deputy Pitt. "Didn't mean to interrupt."

"It's okay," I assured him. "Do you need something?"

I was now standing arm against arm with Eli, and I could feel him stiffen as if preparing himself for a rude response from Pitt.

"Nothing in particular, ma'am," Pitt said, more courteously than he had as yet to talk to me. "I was a little...curt, earlier. No offense meant. I've only been on this job for a week. I was just trying to go by the book."

"No offense taken," I told him and glanced at Eli who seemed a little more at ease now. Pitt hadn't really offended me in any way, but it was polite for him to make sure he hadn't been rude. "We were just leaving."

Eli, Pitt, and I walked out, locking my door and heading for the front entrance. Pitt held the front door open for both of us, and Eli relaxed a little more. I tried my best to hide my grin.

"So, Deputy Pitt," I asked on the way out to the parking lot, "you said you've only been here for a week. Liking it so far?"

He cracked his first real smile I'd seen out of him.

"Yes, ma'am," Pitt answered. "Very nice town. Wasn't expecting a—" his voice trailed off and Eli and I exchanged a glance.

"Well, I wasn't figuring on someone dying so suddenly, in a school no less, first rattle out of the box," he corrected himself.

"Yes, it's a shock," I agreed. "Well, if you have any more questions, you know where to find us."

I gestured toward the school.

He nodded. "But I probably won't be questioning you in particular anymore."

I stopped next to my battered old Jeep Grand Cherokee.

"Well, I did tell you all I knew," I conceded, as I got the door open and tossed my purse in. "I don't know what else you could ask me."

"Oh, it's not that, ma'am," Pitt explained. "Sheriff Darby said he would do the follow-ups with you and your son."

"Why the sheriff?" I asked a question to which I was sure I already knew the answer.

"The sheriff said he would question you two," Pitt repeated. "He didn't tell me why, but Deputy Zindt told me you were the sheriff's sister so—"

I held up a hand to cut him off, unable to avoid Eli's knowing gaze from the corner of my eye. I was disappointed; I had hoped Pitt had apologized out of politeness, but it was looking like he hadn't.

"I will straighten this out with the sheriff," I told him. "And I don't care what Zindt said to you. You weren't rude with us earlier, so there's nothing for you to worry over."

Pitt looked more than slightly relieved. "Yes, ma'am. Thank you. Goodnight," he said and walked away.

Eli went around and got in the passenger side. We lived next door to each other, so we took turns driving each other to school.

"Told you so," he said as he buckled up.

I shot him a level look then, like, don't mess with me. But we both ended up laughing off the tension of the day as we drove home.

CHAPTER 5

It had been one long day at school, and we still needed to get ready for Wednesday night service. I told Eli that I would see him at church, and we parted ways in the front yard.

I walked back out to the mailbox, retrieved the mail, and then dashed back in the house. Another dash up the stairs and I deposited the mail, my purse, and my keys all in a heap on my bed. In about thirty minutes, I was showered and dressed for church. I was applying some mascara to my eyelashes when Darby popped into my bathroom unannounced.

"Ooo! Mama, can I wear some makeup?" Darby begged.

"Did you miraculously get promoted to junior high today?" I asked, holding back a smile.

She turned mopey then. "No, ma'am."

"Then I think you know my answer," I told her, leaning over and kissing her cheek. I gave her a big smile. "But I can sure fix up your hair."

She smiled a little. "Just a ponytail," she said. "We're playing a game outside tonight at church."

"Ponytail it is then."

A few minutes later, we went down to the kitchen where Carter had a bowl of taco soup and a glass of sweet tea waiting on me at the table.

"We ate already, Mom," Carter told me as he was working on one of his chores—taking out the trash. "Didn't know when you'd be home."

"That's fine," I told him right before I prayed over my food. "Any homework?"

"Darby has a little," Carter told me. "But after our day at school, we didn't even get to our afternoon classes. Nobody was worried about homework today."

"True," I conceded. It had been a trying day.

I thought of Ms. Taylor then. If Jess and I were on the correct trek of thinking, why had someone killed her? What purpose would it serve? And she was fairly new in town. Who did she know here that would want to kill her? She was such a nice lady; I couldn't imagine someone being mad enough at her to kill her.

Then there was the comment from the deputy on the phone. She had called the sheriff's department a few days before she died, but about what? Had they done anything when she called? Did she file a report about something, or did she just talk to someone?

Suddenly, I was being shaken.

"What?" I gasped, startled.

"Earth to Mom," Carter said, his hand still on my shoulder. "Are you okay?"

"Yes, yes," I mumbled, trying my best to smile at him. "Just… lost in thought?"

He gave me a curious look but then got back to his chores. He even called out to his sister for her to do her homework since we had enough time before church.

I smiled at ordinary life that had surrounded us again and got back to my supper.

The kids were out the side door, probably already in the Jeep, when I realized I hadn't locked my front door. I made my way back to the front door only to see a figure through the glass in the door. I recognized him, so I pulled the door open.

"Hello, Bo," I told him. "What are you doing here?"

He wasn't my favorite person in the world, but I did usually try my best to be as nice as I could to him.

Bo Blalock had grown up with us, too. Besides Jess, Bess, Eli, and myself, there were two others who taught at the school that had grown up with us as well. Bo was a year older than us, he was Carter's baseball coach and he taught PE and health, and he wasn't much different than he had been in high school—he was still arrogant, and he still liked to pick on people. The other teacher was a quiet guy who was a year younger than us. His name was Gil Pargo, and he taught chemistry.

If I had to choose, I would much rather that Pargo would have been standing on my porch.

"They said you found her," he stated, bluntly.

"Wh—"

"Leigh!" he snapped before I could get a complete word out, stepping closer to me. "You found her body."

He meant Ms. Taylor, of course. Her first name was Leigh.

"Yes," I told him calmly.

His jaw was clenched, and he looked away for a second, over toward Eli's house. I noticed his fists clenching at his sides. It worried me a little—one of my most painful memories from my teenage years included him, so to see him angry near me was, most definitely, *not* comforting.

"Was Flower there?" he asked, looking back at me but nodding his head in the direction of Eli's house.

I couldn't help but roll my eyes when he called Eli Flower. Bo had been a bully in school, and he'd started calling Eli Flower when we were about seven years old and Eli's mom opened a flower shop called Bloom's Blooms.

For a good while, Eli was the little kid, so he never made much of an impact when he fought back to all of the teasing by Bo. Then his mom sent Eli and his brothers to stay with their grandpa the summer after eighth grade—the longest twelve weeks of my life—and when he came back, he had grown a few inches and filled out and continued to grow from there.

He definitely made an impact then!

"No," I said, firmly. "Eli," I told him pointedly, "was upstairs making copies."

"What happened?" he asked, taking another step closer. He was almost in the door frame now, and I had to back up. "She was fine yesterday."

"Your guess is as good as mine, Bo," I told him. "I talked to her right before class, and she was fine then, too."

He seemed ready to rip something apart by then, making me wonder what was up between him and Ms. Taylor. I never saw them talking to each other, but he seemed extremely angry about her death.

"What'd she say?" he asked, looking a little hopeful then. "Did she tell you anything?"

"About what?" I asked. I had no idea what he was talking about.

"When you talked to her," he went on. "What'd she say? Did she tell you—"

"Coach?"

I heard Carter's voice behind me.

Bo looked startled to see Carter.

"Kelley." Bo acknowledged Carter. He called every kid by their last name.

"Are you ok?" Carter asked, stepping up right behind me. "We're on our way to church. You wanna go?"

Bo's demeanor changed quickly. He looked visibly calmer than just a few moments ago, and that made me feel a little better. That and the fact that my overgrown son had shown up.

"Bo, what—?"

"I'm sorry I bothered you, folks," Bo apologized, almost sweetly. He started to back away toward the porch steps. "Kelley, practice tomorrow till five." His glance flitted down to me. "Quinn, I'll see you at school tomorrow. Thanks for the invite."

Then he was gone, and we were left confused, staring after his pickup truck driving away.

"What'd he want?" Carter asked when I shut the front door and locked it.

"I don't know," I told him, a little lost in thought about his comments about Ms. Taylor.

I was still lost in thought as I sat in the passenger seat while Carter drove us to church.

Why was Bo so upset about Ms. Taylor when I had never seen him utter one word to her?

Why'd he show up at my house to ask me about her when he knew I didn't ever truly want to talk to him?

And what in the world did he think she told me?

CHAPTER 6

Church was no less eventful. Worship service wasn't even through the first song, and Miss Mary Larson collapsed on the pew in front of me. I thought my heart stopped for a second.

But she was still breathing, thank the Lord! Eli called an ambulance, and everyone commenced to praying once they realized what happened. The paramedics arrived fairly quickly.

The poor woman was eighty years old and lived by herself. Turned out she had pneumonia and her oxygen dropped too low. She was awake when the paramedics carted her off to the hospital.

No sooner had the ambulance driven away when I saw Borden Carwright, Jess's oldest son, coming out of the men's restroom, his eyes red as if he'd been crying. I didn't see any tears on his face, but his brow was furrowed like a man deep in thought, even though he had only been seven years old for a few days.

I kneeled down on one knee in front of him. I gave him a big smile, hoping it would make him feel better.

"Hey, handsome," I told him, "come here often?"

He just crossed his arms and looked perturbed.

"Okay, honey, what's wrong?" I asked him, when my sweet tactic hadn't worked to pull a smile from him.

"Jackie Robinson," he said, flatly.

"The baseball player?" I asked, confused.

"No, the boy who won't quit picking on me," he informed me indignantly.

"Ah," I said, remembering that Donna, Jess's wife, had told me at some point that a little boy kept picking on Borden about his name.

It brought Bo Blalock to mind, and I wondered if they might be related.

"He keeps calling me Moo and tells everybody that I must belong to a milkman," Borden cried, frustrated. Hot tears were brimming in his bright blue eyes.

The milkman? That was one I hadn't heard in a while, and I couldn't for the life of me figure out how a seven-year-old these days would know what a milkman even was.

"I'm sorry, sweetie," I told him and pulled him into a hug. He clung to me so I lifted him up with me and took him to sit on a bench by a plate glass window that looked out onto the front parking lot of the church.

"Borden, you know your name doesn't have anything to do with milk," I explained. "Louis L'Amour was one of the greatest writers ever, and your grandpa used to read Louis L'Amour books to your dad and your Aunt Bess and me and Uncle Eli all the time when we were kids. We loved it! That's why your dad and Aunt Bess named all their kids after characters from his books."

He sniffled a little. "Yes, ma'am, I know."

I patted his knee. "So don't let him bother you. He's just misinformed. You know your name's special."

He thought about it for a second and then perked up. "I guess it could be worse," he said, finally grinning like the little boy I knew and loved. "My name could be Utah."

My mouth dropped open, but before I could form a response, he hopped off the bench.

"Love you, Aunt Quinn," he said, brightly, as he turned to go.

"Borden, I love you, too, sweetheart, but there's—"

But he was out the door to go out to the playground to join the other kids.

I didn't know what to think. Bess's oldest son was named Utah, and I didn't want her to think I'd told Borden his name was better than any of his cousins. I loved all their names!

I gave an exasperated sigh at the crazy day and stared out the window wondering when this day was ever going to end. I started to get up and go back into the sanctuary then, but something caught my eye.

Without even thinking, I went out the front door and into the parking lot. I could see a few houses down the street, and there was Bo Blalock, banging on the door of a blue house.

"What is his problem?" I muttered to myself as I started walking in his direction.

I stopped at the edge of the parking lot. I didn't want to get too near him, especially since he still seemed angry.

To my surprise, Gil Pargo opened the door. I knew he lived on this street, but I didn't know which house was his. And Gil and Bo were, most definitely, *not* friends.

I was overcome with an overwhelming bout of curiosity, so I started walking down my side of the street. I didn't want them to see me, though. There was really nowhere for me to hide unless I wanted to duck behind the occasional car parked on the street. I kept walking anyway, until I was almost directly across the street from them. Fortunately, I stopped by a tall truck.

"Get off my porch, Blalock!" Gil shouted, forcefully.

That in itself was a great shock to me. Gil had always been so quiet and nice. I'd never heard him raise his voice, and I'd known him ever since he first rode the school bus with me when he started kindergarten. And where were his glasses? I'd never seen him without his glasses either.

"I know she was calling you!" Bo shouted back.

Suddenly, Gil looked up and down the street, so I ducked behind the truck.

What the heck was going on?

I chanced a glance a few seconds later, and they were still on the porch but talking quieter. I couldn't hear anything from them, but they didn't look happy.

Bo poked Gil in the chest, and Gil shoved Bo. I couldn't believe that either—since when did Gil yell at people and go without his glasses and shove people around?

"I mean it, Blalock," Gil said, loudly this time. "Leave now or I'll make you regret it."

My eyes popped round in astonishment.

What in the world was going on with those two?

Bo turned around to leave then, and I had to think fast. My heart jumped into my throat because I didn't want either of them to know that I'd been eavesdropping on them.

I turned quickly and ducked behind a hug oak tree in someone's front yard. I silently prayed they were churchgoers so that they wouldn't be home to see a grown woman lurking and hiding in their yard.

When I heard a vehicle drive away, I waited a few seconds and then headed off in the direction of the church, trying not to walk too fast down the sidewalk.

CHAPTER 7

After we got home from church, I collapsed into bed. I managed to get my shoes off, and that was the last thing I remembered.

I woke up around 1:00 a.m. and sat bolt upright in bed. My bathroom light was on, and a blanket was draped over me. Carter must have covered me up.

Feeling guilty, I trouped over to Darby's room and then Carter's to make sure they were OK. Darby was nestled away, her fish nightlight was aglow. I left her door cracked.

Carter was sprawled facedown haphazard sideways across his bed. One leg was tangled in a sheet, and the comforter was piled off the end of his bed. One pillow was under his stomach, and the other was trapped under his arm that was dangling off the bed.

I smiled to myself, shook my head, and walked out, closing the door behind me. I knew better than to move him; he'd gripe about not getting any sleep in the morning if I did.

Back in my room, I managed to undress and pull on one of John's old T-shirts that I slept in sometimes. I lay back down, pulling up the cover that Carter had put on me.

I thought about John, then, before I dropped back off to sleep. Of all the things I could miss about him, I greatly missed sleeping next to him. But, then again, I missed his smile every morning and his laugh every time I burnt whatever I was cooking.

I had to smile at that. He was a good sport when it came to food—if I made it, he ate it without complaint.

Sleep was almost overwhelming me again after the exhausting day I'd had, so I gave into it. The last thing I saw before I dozed off was the brilliant starry sky outside my window, and it was beautiful. Although, I was quite sure, it wasn't anywhere near as beautiful as what John was experiencing at that same moment.

The next morning, I checked my box in the teacher's lounge while Eli and Bess put their things away. I hadn't taken anything out of it since the week before, so it was pretty full. I immediately started chucking the junk mail.

It was pretty thinned out when I saw the hot pink note card. It had one line of poetry written in very neat block letters: "ROUND ABOUT THE PROW SHE WROTE…"

Tears stung my eyes. *Poor Leigh*, I thought. It had just been a silly little game, but I liked it, and I would miss it. When I got to my room, I slid the note card inside a book of poetry on the shelf behind my desk. I made a mental note to do something with all the note cards from Leigh—they were a memory I didn't want to lose.

A few minutes later Eli, Bess, and I sat over steaming cups of coffee that Bess had brewed in one of her kitchenettes. She was the Family and Consumer Sciences teacher, Home Economics to everyone over thirty, and it was always good when your best friend had full access to kitchens twenty-four hours a day. We never went hungry or thirsty with Bess around.

The coffee was good, especially since we were all pretty well wiped out from the day before.

"So I hear it's better to be named Borden than it is to be named Utah," Bess said as she sipped her coffee.

"Now, Bess, you know I never said—" I started, but she cut me off with a giggle.

"I'm just teasing you," she assured me. "Well, wonder what today holds for us?"

Eli and I sighed at the same time.

"I'm hoping for a big fat nothing," Eli voiced his aspirations for the day.

"Me, too," I told them, and then I thought of Bo and Gil the day before. "Hey, I need to tell y'all something. Eli, will you shut the door?"

A worried look crossed his face, but he got up and closed the door.

"What is it?" Bess asked, wide-eyed.

"You're never going to believe who showed up on my porch last night before church," I told them, still shocked myself.

Eli went stiff in his chair. "Who?"

"Don't blow a gasket," I told him, "but it was Bo Blalock."

Eli was up and out of his chair before either of us could blink an eye. But I managed to jump up and grab his arm, stalling his progress toward the door long enough for Bess to run around both of us and plant herself in front of the door.

"Move, Bess," he ordered, and a look of panic ran across her face. He would never hurt either of us, but he would pick her up and move her if necessary.

"Eli!" I snapped, yanking on his arm and getting around him right before he made it to Bess.

We all stood there a moment, nearly sandwiched together we were so close. I put my hands against his chest, ready to push against him, if need be.

"Please stop, Eli!" I cried. "I need to tell you this. Nothing happened. I'm okay."

I could literally see the wheels turning in his brain. If he could have shot fire from his eyes at that moment, he would have. He was furious, but he needed to calm down.

"Eli, please," I said again, this time quieter and less frantic. "You can't fly off the handle at Bo here. You'll lose your job. I don't want that. The past is the past. But I need to tell you what he said and what I saw later."

Eli was having a harder time than me by leaving the past in the past, but he was calming down, a little. His jaw clenched, and he looked away, but at least he wasn't picking us up and moving us to get out the door anymore.

He looked back to me, then, and covered my hands with his.

"Okay," he said. "For you."

I breathed a sigh of relief, then. He wasn't happy, but he was willing to stop and listen, and I was grateful for that.

Suddenly, for some inexplicable reason, I noticed how strong Eli's chest felt under my hands. I blushed at the thought and averted my gaze. Why in the world had that thought popped into my head?

But then I felt his thumbs rubbing the back of my hands. I looked up again, and he was staring at me. His brow was creased as he studied me, and I blushed all over again. I couldn't find my breath for a second. I—

"Um…" Bess's voice came from behind my head. "Are you two having a moment?"

We jerked away from each other, and Eli stalked back to the desk he'd been in. I reached behind me and pulled Bess back over to the desks to sit, and I told them all that Bo had said on my porch. Then I told them about seeing Bo banging on a door down the street from the church and what I heard and saw when I walked down the street.

"Quinn, have you lost your mind?" Eli snapped at me.

"What?" I snapped back, shocked.

"You followed him?" Eli asked, angry all over again.

I tried to form an answer, but I didn't have one.

"Don't snap at her, Eli," Bess admonished him like she was talking to one of her kids. "But, really, honey," she told me gently, but firmly, "you probably shouldn't have followed Bo. The past is the past, like you said, but you already knew he was angry. Presumably, he was pretty upset over Ms. Taylor, too. Angry upset people do crazy things sometimes."

"I know that," I said, exasperated with both of them for the moment. "But I wanted to know what in the world was going on. I think it's fairly obvious that Ms. Taylor didn't die of natural causes. The police think it's suspicious, then Bo shows up at my house, then Gil and Bo yell at each other. Don't you want to know what's going on?"

Neither one answered for a second or two.

"Yes, I'd like to know," Eli told us. "But not at the expense of your life."

I blushed for a third time that day and dropped my eyes to desk.

"He's right, Quinn," Bess said soothingly, patting my hand. "I don't know what's up with Gil, but Bo can be a loose cannon. We know that all too well."

There was a knock at the door then. We all looked up to see Mattias Shore, Carter's best friend, through the glass in the door.

"I'll hold them off for a few minutes," Bess offered, flashing us both a sly smile.

My heart jumped into my throat.

"Bess," I called after her. "What are—"

But Eli got up, grabbed my hand, and pulled me over to the corner of the room that couldn't be seen from the door.

"Eli, what—"

He held up a hand, and I stopped yet again. "I'm sorry I snapped at you. You're a grown woman perfectly capable of making your own decisions," Eli told me, genuinely looking sorry for his earlier words. "But please look at something from my point of view for just a second?"

He was standing so close that I had to look up at him, and I could smell the soap he'd used that morning. My breath caught in my throat, and I was left wondering why his closeness was beginning to make me notice things about him that had never occurred to me before. We had, quite literally, been best friends our entire lives, so why was it just now hitting me that his soap smelled so good, that his chest and arms looked wonderful in his button-up shirt, and that he was just so darn good-looking.

It didn't help my thought processes any when he gently took one of my hands in his.

"Okay," I told him, near breathless, almost completely oblivious to what he had asked me and ashamed to admit that at the moment I would have agreed to just about anything he asked of me.

"I carried you home one time because Bo Blalock spiked your drink and left you alone with half the football team at a drunken teenage party," he told me. A hurt look ran across his face as he remembered that horrible night from our junior year of high school. I, on the other hand, couldn't remember much past Bo passing me a number of cups of punch. "Jess and I fought six guys just to get you away from them. Bo may not have been one of the ones right there, willing to assault you, but he most certainly set you up."

My face burned, and my chest hurt at the thought. I was embarrassed at having even agreed to go on a date with Bo. I knew he wasn't a nice guy, but I was trying to be a little rebellious at the time—quite contrary to my normal behavior.

It did not end well.

"I'm sorry, too, Eli." I really was. What had I been thinking? "I'm sorry for then and for yesterday."

He offered me a small soft smile and used his other hand to push a few curls behind my ear. And, as if that wasn't enough to make me lose my breath again, his hand slipped behind my head, and he pulled me gently to him, pressing him lips to my forehead.

Dear Lord, I thought, near panic. *Eli just kissed my forehead, and it's wonderful!*

Then he spoke. He still held my hand. His other hand was still immersed in my hair. His lips were still on my forehead. "What would I do if anything happened to you, Quinn?" he breathed against my forehead. "How would I go on without you?"

CHAPTER 8

I spent first, second, and third periods in a daze. My mind was on overload. Ms. Taylor, a young, beautiful, healthy woman, dropped dead right in front of my own son. Then we realize somebody killed her, but we couldn't fathom a reason why.

Next thing I know, Bo Blalock, one of my least favorite people in the world, shows up on my porch and starts questioning me about Ms. Taylor. Then Bo is yelling at Gil, and Gil actually yells back, when I've never heard him raise his voice to anyone since he was five years old.

And the kicker—I am reveling in the fact that the best friend I've ever had just kissed my forehead and held my hand and told me he couldn't go on without me.

What universe had I stumbled into? I wondered, hopelessly confused. For a good ten seconds, I looked around the room for the Cheshire Cat lurking somewhere.

The bell rang, and I nearly jumped out of my skin. The kids started to file out, and I couldn't even remember what I'd said to them that period.

I looked around confused for a few minutes when no kids walked in, but then I realized it was fourth period, my conference period, and I had a stack of papers to copy.

"Get a grip, Quinn," I mumbled to myself, trying to push the thoughts of Ms. Taylor and Gil and Bo and Eli out of my mind for the moment so I could get some work done.

Ms. Taylor's room was still taped off, so her classes were being held in the auditorium. I trouped down the hall and up the stairs with my stack of papers to copy, trying to concentrate on my lessons for the rest of the day.

I managed to get my copies made and just turned to go when Gil Pargo walked in.

I have known this guy all my life, and, at any other time, it wouldn't have bothered me a bit to be in a small space with him. But after I heard him actually yell at Bo the day before, I was a little wary.

But he smiled like he always did.

"Hi, Quinn," he said, just inside the door as it swung closed behind him.

"Hello, Gil," I said, politely, and then I tried to step around him.

But he didn't move.

"How are you?" he asked. "You know, after yesterday. And how's Carter? I heard he was in the room with Leigh."

I nodded trying to ignore the fact that he was blocking the door. I wasn't truly scared of him, but I just didn't know what to think anymore after yesterday.

"We're okay," I told him. "It was a shock. She was very sweet."

A look of nostalgia passed over his face for a second, and then he pushed his glasses up on the bridge of his nose.

"Yes, she was," he agreed, smiling ruefully.

I felt sorry for him then. He looked awfully sad, and while I knew we were a relatively small school, I wasn't aware he knew Ms. Taylor all that well either.

"Gil," I asked, suddenly, "are you okay? Were you two close?"

"Yes," he sighed. "She was my friend."

"Oh, Gil, I didn't know," I told him, patting his arm, surprising my own self since he was making me a little nervous just a few seconds earlier. "I'm sorry."

"Thanks," he said, and then he moved toward the copier.

My hand was on the door handle when his voice stopped me.

"Quinn, don't you usually go to church on Wednesdays?" he asked.

"Yes," I told him, truthfully, half-turning to see him pushing buttons on the copy machine.

He never looked up.

"I thought so," he said. "But I could have sworn I saw you come out of the Barbers's yard last night and start walking off down the street."

"Really?" I asked, trying to sound surprised instead of nervous.

"Yeah." He shrugged, finally looking up at me. "But I didn't have my glasses on, so, you know, probably just someone who looked like you."

I smiled my best. "Yeah, probably," I agreed, making a hasty exit.

I found myself stealing glances at Eli on the way home. It was his turn to drive, so I didn't have to concentrate on the road.

At home, Eli reminded me that we were supposed to all go over to Bess's for supper. The next day was a workday for the teachers, but all the kids would be off, so no one had to be up as early as usual for the next morning.

"I'll come over in about an hour," Eli told me. "I can drive us."

"Okay," I agreed, my throat a little dry.

I couldn't stop thinking about what I'd been trying to avoid thinking all day long—Eli. How was it, that in my entire life, I had never thought of him in the way I was thinking of him now?

Well, for part of the time, I had my answer—John. We met while I was in college, and it didn't take long for me to fall for this sweet man. So for as long as I was with John, I could understand how I hadn't been looking at Eli in any other manner than my best friend.

But what about before I ever met John? Eli and I were always together. Yet if I were being honest, Bess and Jess were always there, too. We joked about how we were the Three Amigos plus one and playfully argued over which one of us was the plus one.

My only explanation was that we were all just so close of friends that anything else never entered my brain. Not until recently, anyway. And only in the last few days had my emotions toward Eli been stirring so differently.

If Eli said anything to me after I had said okay, I didn't know it. I was back in my house, up in my bedroom, without even remembering having gotten out of Eli's truck.

I collapsed onto my bed, kicked off my shoes, and stared at the ceiling.

"Get a grip, Quinn," I told myself for the second time that day.

I sighed and started to get up when paper crinkled under my hand. I looked down to see the mail I'd dumped on my bed the night before; apparently, I had slept right next to it and never realized it was still on the bed.

There was the usual among the pile—phone bill, satellite bill, junk mail. But at the bottom of the pile was a long manila envelope. There was no return address on it, but my name and address were printed on it neatly.

I flipped it over, wondering who had sent it, and opened it up. There was a folded sheet of paper in the envelope along with a folded newspaper clipping.

I unfolded the newspaper clipping first. The clipping included the date which immediately told me that is was twelve years old. The article was on a missing person:

LOCAL TEEN STILL MISSING

Ruby Miriam Doyle, sixteen, was last seen leaving school on the afternoon of March 15. Her older sister, Beth Doyle, eighteen, saw Ruby walk away from the school toward home as she did every afternoon; she never made it home that day. Ruby has been missing for six months.

Ruby was last seen wearing a red T-shirt, with the school's mascot, a cardinal, emblazoned on the front, a pair of black athletic shorts, and white tennis shoes. When Ruby disappeared, she was five feet and seven inches tall and weighed 120 pounds. She has long blond hair and green eyes.

If anyone has any information as to Ruby's whereabouts, please call the local authorities at 555-0101. Ruby's parents, Dr. and Mrs. Philip Doyle, have posted a reward of $20,000 to anyone providing information leading to Ruby's return.

My heart twisted into a knot by the time I finished reading the article. *Those poor people*, I thought. I'd go crazy if Carter or Darby ever disappeared. It would be both horrible and tragic to lose a child, but for a child to just disappear, that was quite another tragedy all its own.

My heart was in for another pain when I opened the folded slip of paper and began to read it.

Quinn,

If you are reading this, I don't believe things ended well for me. But I tried my best. I had to—for Ruby.

My real name isn't Leigh Taylor. It's Beth Ann Doyle, and Ruby was my little sister. I came here to find the man who took her from us. After all these years, I know he didn't just take her—he killed her.

I am sorry for the reasons that brought me to this town, but I'm glad I met you. You are sweet, and I'm glad we are friends.

I hate to ask, but please help me now. If you are reading this, I am no longer able to do anything else to find this man.

He is here in town, possibly even at the school. I don't know what his intentions are these days, but I know they couldn't have been good twelve years ago. No matter what he is doing now, he took my sister away from us, and I have to find justice for her.

Hopefully, this letter is just an overreaction, and I'll be able to talk to you soon. If not, then at least I am with Ruby again.

Be safe and God bless you always.

Your friend,
Leigh

I thought I was going to hyperventilate as I clutched the note. "Oh, my Lord," I gasped, tears stinging my eyes.

Our town? Our school? I thought.

Then Bo and Gil's argument slammed into my head again. Was it one of them? Had one of these people I'd known all my life somehow committed murder?

CHAPTER 9

Still in a state of shock, I scrambled over to my laptop on my desk and booted up my computer. As soon as I could get to the Internet, I quickly typed "Ruby Doyle" and the date of the newspaper clipping in the search bar.

It only took me a few minutes to discover the paper that ran the article. It was called *The Flinch Sentinel*, and it was located in the small town of Flinch, up near Lubbock.

In Sutter, we were deep in East Texas, so anything near Lubbock was several hours away. There was a school system in Flinch. I learned after a few keystrokes that they were a 1A school averaging roughly five hundred kids for the entire district, pre-K through twelfth grade.

I thought about that for a minute. Sutter was a little bigger than that. We averaged about seventy kids per grade level, but we were still a small town. Yet even in Sutter, everyone knew everyone else. If someone disappeared here, we'd be in total shock. We wouldn't be able to fathom anyone we knew kidnapping anyone. And if anyone were new in town, people would know it.

So I could only imagine that in a town as small as Flinch, anyone would be noticeable, especially if they were new. A stranger would be the first person the police went to.

I started scanning the articles on the paper's online archives. The earliest ones never even mentioned anything out of the ordinary. People were questioned, of course, but the names mentioned in the paper were all referred to as longtime residents or family members or friends. They never even mentioned any clues found. I did find one article that said she had a backpack with her that day as well, but there was never any sign of it. More importantly, though, was the mention of a silver necklace with a round silver pendant on it—it was never found either.

It was like Ruby Doyle simply walked into oblivion.

She was there one minute, and then she just wasn't there anymore.

Carter's shout from downstairs startled me.

"It'll be time to go in fifteen minutes, Mom," he bellowed up the stairs at me.

"Okay," I yelled back.

I tucked the clipping and the note back in the envelope and put the envelope in my purse.

I stared at the computer screen as I shut the computer down.

What was I going to do?

This was my first request from beyond the grave; I was quite dumbfounded.

The smart thing to do would be to just hand over the clipping and the letter to my brother—he was the sheriff, after all. But I felt connected to this, and I didn't want to let it drop. She had been my friend, and she had asked for my help.

I, at least, needed to know some more before I handed over anything to the sheriff's department.

Then it dawned on me. Jess's wife, Donna, was from up near Lubbock. They met up there when Jess was away at college at Texas Tech. I could ask Donna and Jess if they knew or remembered anything about Ruby Doyle.

I filed the thought away as I changed my clothes to get ready to go to Bess's house for our fajita supper.

I was still lost in thought when Darby popped into my room a few minutes later. Her appearance pulled me from my thoughts long enough for me to slip my feet into a pair of sandals. I checked the mirror to make sure my clothes matched because when I had changed a few minutes earlier, I had still been lost in a fog.

"C'mon, Mama," Darby prodded, pulling my hand. "Uncle Eli's waiting in the kitchen."

The mention of Eli sent another train of thought through my already cluttered mind.

"Darby, go keep Uncle Eli company for a bit," I told her with a smile and a kiss on her forehead. "Tell him five minutes."

"Okay," she said cheerily and then popped back out of my room.

She loved her Uncle Eli. So did Carter. This was yet another fact that wasn't lost on me—how much my kids already cared for Eli, and Eli felt the same about them.

I dashed into the bathroom. With my curly hair, running a brush through it would only make it stand out in all directions. So I pulled it into a ponytail, and then I applied some mascara.

I made my way back through my room to head downstairs. Eli had seen me dressed to the hilt, makeup perfectly applied, and hair expertly coifed. But he had also seen me at my worst, without a stitch of makeup on, my hair standing on end, or drenched in sweat when we had played baseball years before, or just everyday normal me, my hair in a ponytail wearing a T-shirt and jeans. Sadly, he'd even seen my passed out drunk back when Bo had spiked my drinks and as a puffy red-faced crying mess when John died.

So I didn't know what I was really trying to accomplish by putting my hair up and fixing my face. Eli had seen my worst, my best, and everything in between. His opinion, I was fairly certain, was already set.

The drive out to Bess's gave me some more time to be lost in thought. We stopped to pick up Carter's best friend, Mattias, and then continued on. My house and Eli's house were on a quiet street just a few minutes out of town, but Bess and her family lived on a ranch about twenty minutes out of town.

Coye Wheeler, Bess's husband, came from a long line of ranchers. He was very successful at raising beef, and they had a beautiful place.

We loved to go out there. We'd spend most of our summers swimming in their pool or lounging under the shade trees while the kids played in the pastures. Carter enjoyed helping Coye with the cows and horses. Darby and Noelle, Bess's youngest, were the same age, best friends, and the only girls among out crew of kids.

Eli had never had any kids, but between Jess, Bess, and I, we had a passle. Borden and Chantry were Jess's sons. Bess had two boys, Utah and Finian, and of course, Noelle. My two, Carter and Darby, made five boys and two girls between us all. When you get together with that many kids, plus their other friends, Bess's place was the only one big enough to hold us all.

I smiled at the thought. But I was also saddened by the idea that Ms. Taylor and her little sister would never have families of their own. Ruby Doyle had been gone without a trace for twelve years. Whatever had become of her probably wasn't pleasant, and her poor sister spent years hunting down the culprit who took Ruby. Beth Doyle had changed her name and moved away from her family to find justice for her sister. In the end, though, both sisters were at the mercy of some man who seemingly had no qualms about kidnapping young girls and murdering someone who got too close to the truth.

As Eli turned onto Bess and Coye's long driveway, another thought assaulted my brain. Nobody, except whoever killed her, and I, knew Leigh Taylor was really Beth Doyle. Her parents didn't even know she was dead!

I had to tell them! They had to know!

I didn't want to yet, but I was going to have to tell my brother. He was the law, and I couldn't just let Leigh lie in the morgue at the county coroner's office perpetually waiting for relatives who would never show up.

But I wasn't going to just let it go at that. My mind kicked into overdrive, in a good way at least, for the first time in a few days. Coye had an office with a copy machine where he conducted his ranch business. I'd make a copy of the letter and the clipping to keep.

As soon as we got the kids squared away, I'd slip off to Coye's office and use the copy machine and his computer to see if I could find a number to Dr. and Mrs. Philip Doyle.

CHAPTER 10

Even in my eagerness to get to Coye's office and do what I felt I needed to do, I couldn't help but pause and admire a sight that quite literally brought tears to my eyes.

As soon as Carter barreled out of Eli's backseat, he tackled Eli in a bear hug, both of them laughing and grinning, and then Carter and Mattias took off in the direction of the food. Eli was still grinning when Darby jumped out of the backseat and onto his back.

She held onto him, laughing, and planted a kiss on his cheek.

"I love you, Unc," she squealed, and my heart leapt. I had to look away a moment, blinking several times to clear my vision.

When I looked back, they were both still grinning, heading for the house.

Eli would never be John; their daddy was with the Lord for eternity. But they loved Eli, he loved them, and he would do anything under the sun for us.

I couldn't hide my smile at the thought of Eli and my kids.

Alone on the driveway, trying to catch my breath, I had an epiphany about two completely different situations, a potentially happy and wonderful one and one potentially fraught with dangers.

One: I was falling for the best friend I ever had.

Two: There was a murderer in our midst.

It took me a good half hour to get clear of all the people. Every kid had a friend to say hi to and who wanted to say hi to us. Coye wrapped every person who walked through the door in a hug that could crush a car—his usual greeting for friends and family.

Donna, Jess's wife, and Bess pulled me into the kitchen to show me some new salsa they had concocted. I did, in fact, need to talk to Donna to ask her a few questions about Ruby Doyle, but I needed to make those copies ASAP!

Finally, I was able to extract myself from the kitchen, make it past about a dozen kids ranging in age from five to fifteen, and sidestep all the guys who were out on the huge patio/outdoor kitchen steadily grilling strips of beef and chicken for fajitas.

The bathroom was right next to Coye's office, and I chanced a glance back just to make sure no one saw me. I was out of sight, so I stole past the bathroom door and slipped into Coye's office unnoticed.

A few moments later, I had made two copies of the clipping and two of the letter. I tucked the copies away in my purse and put the originals back in the envelope. I left them out to give to my brother.

Drew, my older brother, and Coye had been friends since we were all kids, too. I was certain Drew would show up at any moment. Bess had mentioned that he had called right before we got there to say he would be late.

I was thankful Coye was still logged onto his computer, so I could surf the net for the Doyle's phone number. I just hoped I hadn't spent too much time in the kitchen with Bess and Donna; Drew could show up at any time.

It only took a few minutes to find out that a home phone number wasn't listed. But Leigh's dad was a doctor in Flinch, Texas. No dice there either, so I broadened my search to the Lubbock area.

And there he was!

Dr. Philip Doyle, optometrist, had an office in a town right outside of Lubbock.

Quick as I could manage, I put the number in my phone. I cleared my search, picked up the envelope and my purse, and headed for the door. When I reached for the doorknob, something caught my eye.

A stack of pictures lay on a table next to the door. In the picture on top of the pile, I recognized a younger Donna standing with a group of girls. They had their arms across each other's shoulders.

Each girl wore a dazzling smile and a medal around their necks. They were standing on a track at a school, which jogged my memory because Donna had went to college on a track scholarship.

I didn't recognize two of the other girls, but one stuck out of the four. Donna was on one end, but on the other end was a slim girl with blond hair, green eyes, and a silver pendant.

I thought I was going to stroke out for a minute. *It can't be*, I thought.

"There's no way," I even whispered to myself. "I'm not looking at who I think I'm looking at."

And, if by some miracle, I was, what was it doing in Bess's house?

I texted Bess; her phone was permanently attached to her person at all times.

COME 2 COYE'S OFFICE ALONE! PLZ!!

Bess appeared in less than sixty seconds. The door swung open, and she looked panicked.

"What?" she gasped. "What is it?"

I pushed the door shut behind her and advised her to lower her voice.

"Why do you have this picture of Donna?" I asked, picking it up and pointing at it. "That's Donna, right?"

She let out a relieved breath and smacked my arm for good measure.

"Is that all?" She looked at it. "Jess and Donna gave me a stack of old photos. I'm putting them in a scrapbook for them. And, yes, that one's Donna."

I stood there flabbergasted for a moment.

"What?" she asked when I didn't respond, looking panic-stricken all over again. "Quinn?"

I had to tell her. So I blurted out everything. I told her about the letter and the clipping, and then I handed her the copies from my purse to read. She was in just as much shock as I was. I reminded her about Bo on my porch, and Bo and Gil's argument, and I told her about running into Gil in the copy room.

"This girl," I said, pointing to the blond girl with the green eyes. "She has got to be Ruby Doyle. She's the right height, build, she has green eyes and blond hair. Look at her jersey. There's a cardinal on it. She's even wearing a silver necklace like the one described in the article I found. Maybe Donna knew her."

"So let's tell Drew," Bess said.

"I am," I told her. "But I want to talk to Donna first. See what she knows. And I want to tell her parents."

Bess looked worried. "Oh, Quinn, you need to let Drew handle this," she advised. "He's the sheriff. He knows how to handle this stuff. Besides, this means, for sure, that there's a murderer at or around the school. He needs to know now."

I sighed knowing she was right. But I was going to talk to Donna, and I was going to call Leigh's parents. Leigh asked me to help because I had been her friend.

Drew would have the letter and the clipping before the night was out, but not before I did what I had to do first.

Bess got Donna into Coye's office, while Bess went out to occupy Drew who had just walked in. It took me a few minutes to fill Donna in on everything. Hurt washed all over her face by the time I was done.

"I knew her," Donna said, closing her eyes and rubbing her forehead. She walked over and sat down in Coye's desk chair clutching the photo. "Beth was here? At the school?"

"Yes," I said, softly. I hadn't realized she'd be this sad. "Did you know them that well? I didn't know. I didn't mean to hurt your—"

"It's okay," she said, sighing. "I only knew them from track. But you kinda get to know people when you see them over and over at track meets. I was a senior in this picture, Beth was a junior, Ruby was a freshman." She gave a short, soft laugh. "Ruby would have been awesome. She kicked our tails that day. She got first, I got second, and Beth and Monica, the other girl here, tied for third."

"Did the police question you back then?" I asked not wanting to bring back painful memories but still curious as to what she might know.

"Kind of," Donna told me. "But she went to Flinch, and I went to Spur. It wasn't like I saw them on a daily basis. They questioned the whole track team at my old school. I was already in college when she disappeared, but there was a track meet the day she disappeared. I went with my coach to watch it; she was checking out Beth because Beth was up for a track scholarship. Ruby ran that day, too, and, dang, could that girl run!"

"Do you remember what you told them?" I prodded further.

She thought about it a minute. "Just that I knew her and Beth from track. Ruby was sweet and nice. I couldn't imagine a reason for her to just disappear…unless someone took her."

I nodded. "Donna, I'm going to call her parents. They need to know. Leigh asked for my help, and I have to tell her parents."

"Parent," Donna corrected me. "Her mom's dead."

"Whose mom is dead?" boomed a voice from the door.

Donna and I both jumped, startled. Drew was standing in the doorway. I could have kicked myself! How was I going to call Dr. Doyle now?

"Donna? Quinn?" he said, in his stern sheriff demeanor. "Who's mom is dead?"

"Beth Doyle," Donna answered. "A girl I knew from high school."

My heart sped up. Donna wasn't lying, and from the look on my brother's face, I was guessing he didn't know who that was yet. He eyed both of us, trying to decide if he believed us or not.

"And Quinn knows her?" he asked, warily.

"Oh, just recently, yes," Donna explained.

She laid the picture down and edged past my brother who still loomed in the doorway.

"I need to go help Bess," she said and was gone.

"What's going on, Quinn?" he asked, still suspicious.

I didn't want to lie, but I wanted to call Leigh's father before my brother did. It was news that would be unbearable, but I thought he should hear it from her friend, rather than the police.

But the opportunity had passed. Drew saw the envelope in my hand, and I couldn't just lie about it.

"Don't be mad at Donna," I told him. "I just kind of ambushed her about it."

I handed him the envelope, and he took it.

"Ambushed her about what?" he asked, opening the envelope.

"You'll see," I assured him, backing away and dropping into Coye's desk chair.

I knew my brother, and I was almost positive he was about to go from wary to irate in five seconds flat.

I watched his face for the few moments it took him to read the article, then the letter. I was right—I knew my brother.

He kicked the door shut with his foot and took a step closer to me.

"Quinn, when did you get this?" he asked, his temper rising.

"I didn't see it until today after school," I told him. "But I got the envelope out of the mail yesterday. I didn't open it then."

"Why didn't you call me?" he demanded.

"I don't know," I told him. "I wanted to help her."

"How?" he cried. "By hoarding evidence?"

"I wasn't hoarding it," I shot back, springing to my feet. "I just wanted to call her parents—"

"You didn't?" he exclaimed, angry and worried all at the same time.

"No," I said, a little quieter.

He sighed in relief.

"I need to take this back to the office, then contact Dr. Doyle," he told me, sternly.

"Okay, okay," I told him, frustrated.

Then it dawned on me all that Bo and Gil had said.

"Uh," I stammered.

"What?" he asked, his aggravation rising. "What is it, Quinn?"

I opened my mouth to tell him but then stopped.

"Why'd you tell Pitt not to question me and Carter anymore?" I changed the subject.

"Zindt told me he was being rude to y'all," Drew said, heatedly.

"And you're not?" I snapped. "If this is not rude, I don't know what is."

He threw his hands up in the air.

"I am not being rude, Quinn!" he exclaimed, exasperated, but less angry. "A woman died. Scratch that. She was murdered. And you get a letter from her saying the man responsible is in this town, possibly at your school. I can only assume that he killed her, so if you stick your nose in this, what do you think he'll do to you?"

I couldn't open my mouth.

"What about Carter and Darby?" he went on. "What would happen to them if something happened to you? Sure, they have plenty of family and friends to take care of them, but nobody could ever replace their mother."

Tears sprang to my eyes. I was still aggravated because he was snapping at me, but he was right. I wanted to help Leigh, but I had to be there for my kids.

The thought that a kidnapper and killer might think I knew something truly sank in then.

"I have to tell you something else," I admitted and then completely filled him in about Gil and Bo.

Drew stiffened at the mention of Bo's name. They were friends once upon a time, but after Bo spiked those drinks on me so long ago, Drew had no use for him. Between Eli and Jess and Drew, there were several guys who thought twice about ever laying a hand on a female.

"I need to go," he told me, pulling me into a fierce hug. "I'm sorry, sis."

"Me too," I said against his chest as I hugged him back.

"I'll call you and Donna later," he told me. "Stay close to a phone."

Then he was gone, and I went back to the crowd of people waiting to eat.

CHAPTER 11

I put on a good face at supper. People were used to Drew running in and out on police business, and Bess and Donna didn't question me further. They knew I'd fill them in when I knew anything further. The food was good, and the kids were still running strong at ten o'clock. The kids had already conspired on who would spend the night with whom.

Eli and I left about 10:15 p.m. and dropped off Carter and Mattias at Mattias' house. Darby stayed with Noelle, of course. That girl stayed at Bess's so much that she had her own corner in Noelle's closet, fully stocked with clothes.

"What's wrong?" Eli finally asked when we pulled into the driveway at his house.

I sighed and looked out the window toward my house. The porch light was on, and the night-light in my bathroom glowed. Suddenly, I thought I should leave more lights on when I left the house.

"I opened a letter from Leigh Taylor today," I confessed, turning to look at him.

"What?" he asked in shock.

I filled him in on all he didn't know—the letter, the article, scanning the Internet about the Doyles, talking to Donna, and fessing up to Drew. His expression was full of concern, but I could tell he was aggravated with me again.

"Quinn, I said earlier that you were a grown woman," he admitted, "and you are. But I'm glad Drew stopped you. If you had called that poor man, you don't know how he would have reacted. And what about holding onto the letter and the article? If Drew wasn't your brother, you might have been slapped with obstructing justice or some such charge."

I sighed again and leaned my head back against the seat. I honestly had just seen the letter that afternoon, so I really wasn't going to hang onto it that long. But Drew probably wouldn't be too happy with the fact that I had made copies.

"I know, Eli," I conceded as I stared at the roof. "I just wanted to help the girl somehow. She was already gone because she was getting too close to finding out who took her sister. I didn't want her body to just lie in the morgue, unclaimed."

Eli started to speak, but I cut him off.

"I know Drew would have contacted the family after I gave him the letter," I told him. I wasn't aggravated with Eli; I was just aggravated with the whole situation. "She asked me, Eli. I just…wanted to be sure she wasn't forgotten."

I was still staring at the roof when I felt his hand cover mine. At any other point in our lives, I would have just thought Eli was trying to comfort me, but now something in me stirred. I tried to take a breath, but it caught in my throat.

I was glad it was fairly dark in the truck because I knew I was blushing.

"Quinn," he said, softly, slipping his fingers in between mine.

"Yes?" I managed to eek out.

He was quiet for a minute while my heart hammered against my chest.

"Are you going to stare at the roof all night?" he asked, a little amusement in his voice.

"Oh…" I couldn't look at him. "I was contemplating it."

He laughed then, and it eased my nerves a little.

"C'mon," he said, letting his hand slip from mine as he opened his door. "I'll walk you to your door."

He was around the truck and opening my door before I could respond. He opened the door and held out his hand. I took it, and he shut the door behind me, pulling me toward my house. I stared at our hands clasped together as we walked the few feet over to my side door.

I fished my keys out of my purse and unlocked the door. I opened the door, reached in to turn on the light, immediately turning back to Eli.

"Thanks," I told him. "I'll drive tomorrow. We don't have to be at school 'til ten, thank the Lord."

He agreed with my thanks and smiled, and I thought my heart might melt. I almost lost my senses at that smile.

"See you at nine thirty then," he told me, stepping up on the step below the one I stood on. My breath caught in my throat again.

He leaned in and gave me peck on the cheek. It wasn't the first time he'd ever done that, but it was most definitely the first time butterflies danced in my stomach when he kissed my cheek.

He pulled back and smiled at me. "I just want you to be safe, Quinn," he told me. "Let Drew handle finding the bad guy."

"Okay." I couldn't do anything but agree with him at that point.

He backed away as I stared after him and then turned on his heel and headed over into his yard.

Inside the kitchen, I leaned against the door I had just locked. My head was filled with too many thoughts. I hoped Drew could help find who killed Ms. Taylor, kidnapped, and presumably done away with, her sister. I wanted justice for both of them.

On the complete and opposite end of the spectrum, I had to admit what all these feelings about Eli meant. Nothing like my recent thoughts of Eli had entered my mind since John. But it had been nearly three years since he had died. I had loved John so much, I always would, but he was gone, and I was still here.

But now...

Now, I thought nothing in the world sounded better than a smile or a hug or a kiss from Eli Bloom.

I made sure the doors and windows downstairs were locked, and then I headed up to bed. At the top of the stairs, I knew something was wrong.

I stopped, my hand still on the bannister. There was a lamp on in Darby's room, and it shone into the hall through her open door. But that wasn't enough to illuminate the whole upstairs hall.

I peered through the dimness into my room. The night-light that glowed in my bathroom wasn't right. I hadn't left my bedroom door open all the way like that.

Then the idea of a killer around here crept across my brain.

I turned to go back down the stairs, but a shadow moved in my room, and I was momentarily shocked. When it moved again, I was spurred into movement once more.

I tried to move quietly down the stairs, but then I heard footsteps behind me, and I panicked. I jumped from the fourth step up and yelled for Eli at the top of my lungs.

When I landed, I stumbled a step but regained my footing and scrambled for the kitchen door.

"Eli!" I screamed again.

I didn't look back. I scrambled at the lock on the back door, managing to get it unlocked and open just as I felt a strong hand on my arm.

The hand squeezed my upper arm, but I threw myself forward out the door, screaming for Eli yet again as I fell out into the side yard.

"Quinn!" I heard the next second, accompanied by pounding feet.

I was sprawled on the ground, face-first, so I flipped over. There was a dark figure in the doorway. Eyes looked down at me from a ski mask that concealed the figure's face.

The figure turned back into the house and was gone from sight just as Eli skidded to a stop beside me. He helped me up, and I clung to him.

"Your house, Eli," I breathed out in a ragged breath, my chest aching from my heart hammering so hard against it. "Please."

He put his arm around me to lead me back to his house, but my knees began to buckle before we reached the porch.

My head swam, and I tried to get a good breath as my heart pounded too hard and too fast. I grabbed at forming a cohesive thought, but a fog settled over my mind, and I drifted away.

*****

"Quinn?"

It sounded like my brother, but I couldn't be sure.

"Quinn?"

It was definitely my brother.

"Go away, Drew," I mumbled. "It's not time to get up yet."

He laughed.

"Yes, it is, kid," he told me, and then he shook my shoulder softly. "Quinn?"

My eyes popped open. Drew was sitting next to me, and we weren't in my old bedroom back at my mom and dad's. I was on Eli's couch.

"Eli!" I cried out, sitting bold upright.

I plopped back on the couch cushions immediately. My head was still swimming.

"What happened?" I moaned with my hands over my face.

"You fainted," Drew explained. "But we'd like to know what happened before that."

I uncovered my face to see Eli sitting on the coffee table now. He looked sick with worry.

Without even thinking, I reached out and grabbed his hand. He held my hand tight and smiled at me.

Drew looked back and forth between us and then honed in on me.

"What happened, Quinn?"

"Someone was in my bedroom," I told him. "They chased me down the stairs. I felt a hand grip my arm just as I flung myself out the side door."

I stopped for a second.

Someone was in my house!

"Quinn?" my brother prodded.

"I saw a dark figure standing in the doorway, after I fell out in the yard," I went on. "Dark clothes. Ski mask. It had to be a man. The figure was built like a man. Eli came running up, and the guy turned back into the house."

"I got her up off the ground as soon as I got to her," Eli told Drew. "I carried her in here and called you."

Drew nodded. "We're combing the house now. Your room's been tossed, but the rest of the house looks in order. My guys will be over there a while."

"I'll just stay on this couch," I told him, flatly. "I don't feel so well. You know where to find me if you need me."

"Okay," Drew said and then looked between me and Eli again. When he stood up, he looked pointedly at Eli. "Behave."

Eli's mouth dropped open, but then Drew was gone in another of his famous hasty exits.

CHAPTER 12

Pitt came and asked me the same questions two different times while Drew and some other deputies were over at my house taking pictures and fingerprints. When I had walked in on the prowler, it had been about a quarter to eleven. Drew and his deputies didn't clear out until almost 2:00 a.m. I had been dozing on and off on the couch, in between Pitt's questions; Eli was trying to sleep in his recliner.

Finally, when the last of them headed out, I told him to go to bed.

"No, I'll stay here with you," he said, sleepy-eyed, trying to settle back into his recliner.

"Eli, I'm fine," I assured him. "Go to bed. We're already going to be dragging in the morning."

"I'm not leaving you by yourself," he said, very firmly. It was his final word on the matter, and there was no doubting that.

But I wasn't going to let him suffer all night in a recliner.

I threw back the blanket I'd been covered in and stood up carefully. I had been a little light-headed earlier, and I didn't want my head swimming again. I reached my hand out to him.

"Quinn—" he was wide-eyed, and I couldn't help but smile a little at his look of panic.

"It's okay, I won't steal your virtue," I teased him.

His neck turned red, but he didn't hesitate to stand up and take my hand.

I led him to the spare bedroom and picked up the blanket that lay across the foot of the bed.

"Here." I handed it to him. "Which side do you usually sleep on?"

"The left," he said, looking confused.

So I walked to the right side, pulled the comforter back, and crawled in, pulling the covers back up over me. I patted the top of the comforter on the left side of the bed.

"Now you'll be in the same room with me, and we can get some sleep," I explained.

He didn't know what to say, but he kicked off his shoes and lay down on top of the comforter and covered up with the quilt that I'd handed him. He lay on his back, his hands behind his head, his gaze trained on the ceiling. I snuggled into the comforter on my side facing him.

I was nearly out again when I heard my name.

"Yes?" I whispered without opening my eyes.

"If your brother comes back, he's going to shoot me," he whispered.

"Probably," I whispered back with a giggle.

In a second or two, he let out a nervous laugh. I smiled to myself, and a few seconds after that, I was asleep.

A few hours later, sunlight spilled into the room, pulling me from my sleep. *I wouldn't open my eyes*, I told myself. I hadn't had enough sleep.

An arm around my shoulder caused my eyes to fly open. My head was on someone's chest, my left arm stretched across their midsection.

Don't move, I told myself. It might be a dream.

But I had to look up.

Slowly, I lifted my head to see Eli's sleeping face.

My heart begged to melt all over again. I laid my head back down and closed my eyes reveling in the moment.

I definitely would not be moving again until he did.

"Quinn."

I heard my name, but I didn't want to wake up again.

"It's eight o'clock."

I didn't want to get up. Not now. I just wanted to lie there without moving or thinking.

But my eyes fluttered open anyway. I was still as I was before. Eli's arm was around my shoulders as I rested my head on his chest, my left arm stretched out across him.

"I don't want to move, Eli," I confessed, without looking at him.

I could hear his heart beat a little faster under my ear.

"You don't?" he asked, quietly.

"No," I said, snuggling closer to him but still not looking at his face. I was in uncharted territory here. I was pretty sure he was having the same kind of feelings about me, but I couldn't read his mind—I didn't know for sure.

He squeezed my shoulder, then. "Me either, Quinn."

I smiled, burying my face against his chest. It was comforting to know that he wanted to hold onto me as much as I wanted to hold onto him.

But I didn't know what else to say at that point. I didn't know how to broach the subject of falling for my best friend. And, truly, he hadn't spoken any words to me that said he was absolutely falling for me, too. But, still, one could tell by his actions and by the things that he *had* said to me here lately that his feelings were more than just concern for a dear friend.

Then he spoke, breaking the silence.

"Please, look at me," he said, softly.

My heart jumped in my throat, but I did it. I pulled my head back enough to look at him.

"I need to tell you something," he said, and then he shifted his weight, pulling us both up into a sitting position.

He smiled and took both of my hands in his. I could feel my face flush, but I couldn't look away from him.

"What is it?" I managed to say, although I didn't know *how* I had managed to say it.

"As my friend," he began, "I have loved you and cared for you my entire life. But I don't want to just be your friend anymore."

My breath caught again, and I looked away out the window. I could see my house across the yard; it brought Carter and Darby to mind. I was elated by his words, but I wasn't alone. I had to consider what they might want. Oh, I knew they loved Eli, but I had to say something to them, figure out how they might be affected by the situation.

"Quinn," he said, as I stared out the window.

I surprised both of us by turning and flinging my arms around him. I buried my face against his neck, hugging him and holding on for dear life. After a startled second, he wrapped his strong arms around me.

"Does that mean you feel the same way?" he asked, unable to keep a small chuckle out of his voice.

I laughed against his neck and pulled back to look at him again.

"Yes," I assured him. "But I need to talk to Carter and Darby. I can't just think about me. I—"

"You don't have to explain," he said, his voice full of understanding. "I'm not trying to push you into anything. I just needed you to know how I felt. I just couldn't hold it in anymore."

"Good," I told him, "good."

Then I was hit suddenly by a wave of panic. "What do I say to them, Eli?"

He pretended to seriously think about it for a second and then cracked a grin. "Tell them tall, dark, and handsome from next door is in love with their mother."

I slapped his arm as we both laughed at his suggestion. But as we got up to head over to my house, so I could shower and change, I couldn't get the words 'in love' out of my head.

CHAPTER 13

My room had indeed been "tossed." But I tried my best to ignore the disarray and the fingerprint dust and snagged my toothbrush and some clothes to go shower in the kids' bathroom. Drew had given us the okay to go back in the house—they had taken pictures and gathered evidence until nearly 2:00 a.m., but my room felt strange somehow.

Later, we pulled into the parking lot at school five minutes to ten. We headed to my room, and Eli shut the door behind us.

"I'm pretty sure the guy in your house means somebody knows Leigh sent you a letter," Eli said as I locked my purse in my filing cabinet.

I plopped down in my desk chair as the knowledge sank in. But how would anyone know?

"I told Bess, Donna, you, and Drew," I told him. "None of y'all are going to send a masked man to ransack my bedroom."

"True," he admitted.

"So how did they know?" I countered.

"I don't know, but it worries me," Eli said, honestly. "With Ms. Taylor dying and Bo confronting you and the letter, it all has to lead up to the masked man somehow."

I nodded. "Yeah, it can't be a coincidence at this point."

After a silent moment, he asked, "Was anything missing?"

I sighed. "Honestly, I didn't look. It…bothered me to even be in there this morning. Anyway, since it most likely wasn't just some random prowler, what would be missing?"

"Well, they had to have known Leigh wrote you that letter," Eli explained.

"Yeah," I agreed, following his train of thought. "So—"

"So I think they were after whatever else they believe she sent you."

"There was nothing else," I cried as soon as he said it.

But the principal, Mr. Scott, knocked on the door just then. I went over and opened it.

"Sir?" I asked, but he only nodded to me and then looked directly at Eli.

"Mr. Bloom," Mr. Scott said, "you need to report to the library."

"Now?" Eli asked, standing up.

"Now," Mr. Scott confirmed.

"Yes, sir," Eli said, and then he turned to me. "Talk to you later, Quinn."

I felt his hand trail across the small of my back as he walked by. I wanted to pull him back, but we were at work, and there were things I needed to talk out with my kids before we tried to start anything new for us.

Then, a slight panic washed over me. What if they didn't want me and Eli to be anything more than friends? I couldn't imagine that, but what if?

"Ms. Kelley," Mr. Scott said, rather loudly.

I jumped. "Sir?"

He cracked a rare smile. "Are you alright?" he asked. "I called your name, but you were lost in thought."

I smiled, slightly embarrassed. "Oh yes, sir. I'm fine."

"I wanted to thank you again for helping with the students on Wednesday," he said. "I know it must have been quite a shock to find Ms. Taylor like that. And, Carter? How is he? He was in the room?"

"Yes, he was," I confirmed. "But we're okay, and I just did what I could to keep the kids calm."

He nodded. "Thank you anyway. I'll leave you to your work."

"Okay," I said as he walked off. I made my way back to my desk and plopped down again.

Bess was through my door swinging it shut behind her before I could turn my computer on. She sailed to the student desk nearest to me.

"A masked man was in your house? Why didn't you call me?" she asked, aghast at the fact that I hadn't filled her in immediately.

I smiled at my friend.

"Sorry," I told her, "but you had your hands full with all the kids. I'm okay. Eli came to my rescue."

She grinned. "He did?"

I tried not to look at her grin, but I couldn't hide my smile.

"Quinn," she said, slowly, pronouncing every letter. "Spill, girl."

"Bess, I—"

"Spill the truth," she practically ordered inching forward in her seat.

"Well…" *Where do I start?* I thought. Bess and I told each other everything, so it was going to come out. This was just a conversation I had never expected to have with her.

I decided to shock her right off the bat.

"We slept in the same bed last night," I said, bluntly.

Her mouth dropped open, and she nearly fell out of the chair. I couldn't hold back the laughter.

"Quinn Kelley," Bess said sternly. "You did not—"

I held up my hand before she finished her sentence.

"No," I assured her, recovering from my burst of laughter. "I'm just messing with you."

Her hand clasped at her neck as she sighed in relief, and I explained about the man in the house, and Eli helping me over to his house.

"After Drew and his deputies left, Eli didn't want to leave me alone, and I didn't want him to try to sleep in a lumpy, old recliner," I explained. "We went to the spare bedroom, and I got under the covers. Eli slept on top of the covers with the spare blanket. It was perfectly innocent and harmless."

Her smile returned, but it was laced with concern.

"Sure you're okay?" she asked.

I turned the question over in my head. "Yes," I assured her. "Eli told me something this morning."

Her concerned smile turned to a goofy grin.

"Let me guess," she announced, sitting up straighter, trying to look her most professional. "I love you, Quinn Darby Kelley, and I cannot live without you." She paused to check my expression. "Am I right?"

"Kind of," I admitted, shaking my head. "How'd you know?"

She was greatly shocked by that question. "How'd I know?" she asked, incredulous. "Quinn, you and I have been attached at the hip, along with Eli and Jess, since birth. When it comes to the three of you, I know it all. The more appropriate question is, how didn't you know?"

I tried to think about that. I had already wondered how I never thought of him as anything other than my best friend. But I didn't have an answer for how I didn't know how he felt about me.

"I don't know," I told her, truthfully, and then I had a thought about what she said. "So, Miss I-Know-Everything-About-You… how do I feel?"

"About Eli?" she clarified.

"Well, of course!" I cried. "Start with the easy stuff, and then we can move onto the really hard subjects like what I want for supper."

She rolled her eyes at my sarcasm.

"You love him," Bess told me, bluntly, amusement replaced by seriousness. "You haven't said it out loud, but you do. It's been boggling your mind because the two of you have been the best of friends, but you are in love with him."

She got up and came around the desk to lean over me, grabbed my shoulders, and pinned me with a direct stare.

"You love him just as much as you ever loved John," she told me, and the words brought tears to my eyes. "I know, sweetie, I know that's difficult to hear, but it won't be for long. God gave you John for a time—to be your husband, your heart, to give you Carter and Darby, to love you and give you many precious memories. But He also gave you Eli, to be your friend, a comfort when no one else would do, and, eventually, for you to be able to love again."

The tears rolled out, and my breaths came faster. She knelt down in front of me when I couldn't speak and took my hands in hers.

"I also know you're worried about Carter and Darby, but you don't need to be," she went on. "They love Eli as much as you do. Discuss it with them, but don't worry. It's going to work out just fine."

"Really?" was all I could manage to say.

The playfulness returned to her face.

"Yes, really," she told me.

She was right. I didn't have any explanation for her explanations, but I just knew she was right.

"And for supper you're contemplating fettuccine Alfredo," she added with a grin. "It's your go-to meal after a stressful situation."

I shoved her shoulder and laughed. "Show off!"

CHAPTER 14

After an hour of working in my room, grading papers and putting grades in the computer, I still hadn't seen Eli come back to his room. I had a perfect view of the hall, and the only person I'd seen since Bess left was Mr. Moss, the Spanish teacher.

I turned in my rolling chair to the bookshelf behind my desk to put back the book I had just been using, and the book of poetry caught my eye. I put down the book I had in my hand and picked up the book of poetry. It opened easily to the page where I had stowed the note cards.

They were all different color, some of them decorated. The last one she'd given me was bright pink, and I considered the line written there. I smiled. I would know that line anywhere—it was from "The Lady of Shallot," my favorite poem.

The note card from about three weeks ago was neon yellow and had silver glitter glue bordering the whole card. This one had been a little tricky. If I didn't get it right on the first try, I had to buy her a cappuccino from the Exxon down the street. She had to buy me a Dr. Pepper if I guessed right on the first try. With the neon yellow card, I had to buy her a cappuccino, but I knew the answer by my second guess.

The line read "I found a thing to do, and all her hair..." It was from "Porphyria's Lover," which, coincidentally, was about an obsessed and disturbed man who strangles his lover. I shuddered involuntarily at the thought and replaced the cards in the book and put the book on the shelf. I needed to get back to work.

A few minutes later, I was at the back of the room putting some graded papers away, when I heard a rap on the door.

"Come in," I said without thinking. My back was to the door, and when I spun around, I came face-to-face with Bo Blalock.

I jumped, literally, and took a step back.

"I didn't break into your house," he said, less than courteous.

That rankled me. I hadn't accused him of anything.

"I never said you did," I shot back. "Don't come in my room and snap at me."

He ignored my last comment.

"So why is your brother calling men to the library and questioning them?" he asked, just as gruffly as he had already spoken.

I was taken aback. Eli was called to the library. That was odd, but then Leigh's letter came to mind. It said the man who took Ruby was at or near this school. Drew must have started questioning everyone. I was glad he was going ahead with the investigation, but I was concerned as to why he was questioning Eli.

Bo Blalock was quite another story. I fully believe people are innocent until proven guilty, but Bo had me worried. I had a natural distrust of him that went way back, but those thoughts aside, he had showed up at my house, questioning me about Leigh.

"He's doing his job, Bo," I said, finally pulling myself from my thoughts. "Leigh died, then someone breaks into my house. He's going to question people."

"I didn't have anything to do with her death or your prowler," he said, firmly.

"Like I said," I reiterated, "I never said you did. But while we're on the subject, why did you show up on my porch questioning me about her?"

He sighed, aggravated, running his hands through his hair.

"I was upset." His words were still forceful, but he was more upset now than angry. "I just want to know what happened to her. We...we were together."

My eyebrows shot up in surprise, and my mouth dropped open.

"What?" I asked, when I regained some composure. "Together?"

"Well, don't look so surprised." He was angry again. "Not everybody thinks of me like you and your friends. You know, for a bunch of Christians, you're awful unforgiving."

That hit me. Hard.

Had we really been giving a bad example to him all these years? I hadn't meant to seem unforgiving; I was just hurt. A few of those guys were friends with Drew, Jess, and Eli, so it hurt to know that they tried to take advantage of me.

"Bo, you spiked my drink so your friends could have their way with me," I said, flatly.

"No," he shot back. "I did not. But you and Drew and Jess and Eli would never listen to me back then."

That tidbit of information was more shocking than Bo admitting he was with Leigh. The whole situation with Bo had turned out to be a swept-under-the-rug situation. We had all ended up at a party flowing with booze, and as scared kids, we didn't want to get into trouble. I was embarrassed, and I didn't want to have to fess up to my parents. In the end, I begged my brother and my friends not to say anything. They didn't—not to our parents—anyway. They did, on the other hand, have a few choice words with the boys involved. They also provided those same boys with several black eyes and bloody noses.

I took a deep breath, not believing what I was about to say.

"Okay, Bo," I said. "I'm listening now."

He had started pacing from agitation, but he stopped and looked at me blankly.

"What?"

"I'm listening," I said, again. "What happened at that party eighteen years ago?"

He still looked stunned, but he finally spoke.

"Not what you think," he started off. His voice rewound the last eighteen years, and I could see him out by the field house where Drew cornered him. They were friends, and Drew was beyond irate that the people who were supposed to be his friends had tried to assault his sister. Bo had tried to talk to us that day, but there wasn't one of us who was ready to listen. After Drew knocked Bo around that day, Bo never tried to talk to us again.

"The punch was spiked, but I thought you knew that," he explained. "We were at a party where everyone was drinking. I gave you the punch, but I was drinking it, too."

He stopped, but I didn't open my mouth. I was going to hear him out.

"I wanted you to loosen up," he admitted, without looking away. I felt my neck go red, but I kept my composure and continued to listen. "And I know I wasn't the best kid, but I would never try to force myself on anyone." He paused for a second. "We were both drunk, but we were alone. I wasn't trying to set you up. Somebody walked up and started talking to me. That's the last thing I remember until I woke up in the middle of the night, laid out in the yard."

He seemed to be finished with his story. He lost some of the arrogance he always seemed to carry around with him. As bad as I hated to admit it, I thought he was being truthful with me. But I also didn't hear any apology in there for what he *had* done. He admitted he wanted me to loosen up and it had, most definitely, not been for wholesome reasons.

I sighed. "Okay, Bo," I told him. "I don't know why you would lie after all these years. I believe what you're telling me. But you still—"

He held up his hand. "I know," he said. "I still had bad intentions, and I'm sorry for that."

I thought I was going to fall over. Bo wasn't one to apologize about anything.

"Thank you," I said, feeling some of the pent-up tension in my bones ebb away. "And I'm sorry if we were guilty of holding a grudge. You're right to say we should be more forgiving. But we're still human, and it was a hurtful situation, and, until just now, I never knew you were sorry about any of it."

He nodded, finally having to look away. He started pacing again.

"I wasn't in your house, and I just want to figure out what happened to Leigh," he said. He was a little less gruff than before, but Bo would always be Bo. I may have believed him, but I doubted we were ever going to be friends. I could forgive him and deal with him, but I would, most likely, never be truly comfortable around him.

"I want to know what happened to her, too," I admitted. "As for Drew, just answer all his questions truthfully."

"I did."

"Good," I said, and he stopped pacing to look at me. "But now if you'll excuse me, I've still got lesson plans to work on."

He nodded and, without another word, walked out.

CHAPTER 15

Following Bo's exit, I left, making sure my keys were in my pocket and that my door was locked. Across the hall, Eli's room was still dark, so I decided to go to the library to see if he was still there. I couldn't imagine why Drew had him down there so long.

As I rounded the corner and came into view of the library doors, I saw Deputy Zindt standing guard outside the doors. I knew immediately that I wasn't getting in that way.

Zindt had asked me out a few times, but I had turned him down. He had probably told Drew that Pitt was being rude just so I'd think he was doing me a favor. That was not the case, though. Sadly, if I wanted to go flirt with him, he'd probably let me in, but that was not about to happen.

He perked up a little and smiled as I came closer.

"Ms. Kelley," he said, nodding at me. "How are you?"

I didn't stop walking, but I managed a nice smile.

"Hello, Deputy," I told him as I passed by.

"Are you okay?" he asked when my back was to him.

I couldn't just ignore him, so I turned around, smile in place, to answer him.

"Yes, thank you," I said, sweetly. "I was just fortunate that Eli lives so close and that y'all showed up so quickly."

His smile broadened. "All part of the job, ma'am."

I turned and kept walking before he could say anything else. I didn't have any real reason to be bothered by him, but he was just the type of guy to mistake friendliness for something else.

I rounded the next corner just past the library and headed for the janitor's closet. There was a door in there that led to the second floor of the library. We were a relatively small school, but a few years back, a bond had passed to build a new library; the old one was remodeled and turned into two new classrooms and a distance learning lab. Part of what was now the upper level of library used to be a storage room used by the janitors. They left the janitor's access to what was now the stacks on the upper level so they could clean upstairs even when there was a class in the main open area in the lower level of the library.

I must have been having a blessed day because the janitor's closet and the door to the stairs were unlocked. At the top of the stairs, I peeked out into the stacks, and I didn't see anyone else up there. The coast looked pretty clear, so I eased the door open and stepped through.

But as soon as I turned to ease the door back shut, all thoughts of blessings flew away, and my heart beat furiously in my chest when a hand clamped over my mouth.

"Don't scream." It was a whisper in my ear from a familiar voice. "It's me."

The hand dropped, and I spun around.

"Eli!" I whispered, sharply. "You scared me half to death."

He put his fingers to his lips.

"It echoes up here," he said as low as he could and still be heard. "C'mon."

He grabbed my hand and led me to one of the aisles in the stacks. The lights were out on the upper level since there were no kids here today. But the lights were on downstairs, and the huge windows across from us on the opposite wall let in plenty of sunshine from outside.

The library was circular, and the stacks we were in only covered about a third of the circle. The rest of the circle was open from floor to ceiling with desks out in the center, the restrooms to the left of us, and the door and circulation desk to the right. More stacks were downstairs arranged around the tables.

Suddenly, Eli dropped to his belly on the floor pulling me down with him. He put his fingers to his lips again and then pointed downstairs. We belly crawled like soldiers in battle as close to the edge of the upper level as we dared.

"Where were you on Wednesday?"

That was my brother's voice. I didn't dare pop my head up. Eli and I kept our heads down with our ears craned toward the voices.

"Here at school. You know that, Drew."

I knew that voice, too. It was Gil Pargo.

"Yes, I know that. But I need you to answer all of my questions."

There was a loud sigh from below.

"So did you see Leigh on Wednesday?" my brother asked.

"Yes," Gil said, "I saw her as I walked in the front door to come to work that morning. She walked in right behind me. I remember holding the door for her. Check the front door camera. We'll be on there right around 7:30 a.m."

"One of my deputies is checking all the cameras as we speak," Drew assured Gil. "Did you see her any other time of the day?"

"Yes."

A pause.

"When?" Drew demanded.

"At lunchtime," Gil went on. "I saw her go in Blalock's room and shut the door."

"Did you see Bo?"

"No," Gil answered.

"Did you see Bo at any time on Wednesday?"

There was only a slight pause, and then Gil answered, "No."

My mouth dropped open. That was a lie! They were yelling at each other on Gil's porch Wednesday night. I shot Eli a confused look, but he just shrugged. Neither one of us knew exactly why Gil was lying. With all that was going on, I could guess why he'd lie. But I couldn't just flat out accuse him of anything.

"Are you sure?" Drew persisted. "Lying to the police is highly illegal. You could be in danger of losing your teaching license if I arrest your for obstruction of justice. I'd hate to—"

"Okay, Drew!" Gil exclaimed.

"After school, Bo came to my house, banging on my door," Gil fessed up. "He said he knew Leigh was calling me. I told him to get off my porch. He demanded to know why she was calling me. I told him to mind his own business, and he let out a few expletives, insulting me. Then—"

Gil stopped, and I so wanted to look over the railing to see both their expressions, but I didn't dare.

"Then what?" Drew pressed for an answer.

"Then I told him to leave or I'd make him regret it," Gil admitted.

"Oh really?" Drew asked, his voice sounding a little surprised.

We all knew Gil; he was quiet and soft-spoken, so surprise was a natural reaction to Gil threatening people.

"And just why did you say that?" Drew prodded.

Gil sighed again. "I just wanted him to go away. I was upset."

"About Leigh?" Drew continued on.

"In a way," Gil admitted.

"In a way?" Drew questioned, using Gil's own words.

"Yes," Gil confirmed. "In a way, I was upset about Leigh. But mostly I was upset because my cousin had died that day."

"Your cousin?" Drew sounded surprised on that one.

"Yes." Gil paused yet again. "My cousin, Beth Doyle."

CHAPTER 16

Eli and I both gaped at each other. They were cousins! So Gil knew the whole time that Leigh Taylor was really Beth Doyle! I fought every urge in me that was yelling to look down at my brother and Gil. Eli could see the wheels turning in my head, and he put his hand on my back to make sure I didn't pop up for a look.

"Look, I'm not stupid, Drew," Gil started again. "I heard the kids say what she looked like when she died. I know part of the reason you're questioning me is because she might have been poisoned, and I'm the Chemistry teacher. I'm sure, in the eyes of the police, that puts a big neon sign on me as a suspect."

Drew started to say something, but Gil cut him off. I couldn't see them, but I bet that didn't sit well with my brother. Drew did not like to be interrupted, especially when it came to police matters.

"I also know that this school is full of people who have access to each other all day long," Gil explained. "Just because I'm the Chemistry teacher doesn't make me guilty."

There was a pause.

"True," Drew admitted. "But you knew who she was and what she was doing here the whole time. So you two do have a connection, and I am going to check every angle."

"I understand."

"Why don't you and I go down to my office and continue this conversation?"

"Are you arresting me?" Gil sounded a little panicked.

There was yet another pause.

73

"No," Drew said. "Not at the moment. But we need to talk."

"Okay," Gil said. "Besides Uncle Philip, I'm sure I want to find out what happened to Beth more than anyone."

Eli and I made a hasty quiet exit back through the janitor's closet. We went back to his room and shut the door behind us.

"Oh, my Lord!" I exclaimed once inside his room. "I thought what Bo told me was shocking!"

"Really?" Eli asked.

"Yes, and you know what?" I asked, confused. "I haven't told anyone what he told me."

"Was it about Bo and Leigh being a couple?" he asked.

"Partly," I conceded. "But how—"

"After Drew questioned me, I saw Bo going in," Eli explained. "I went through the janitor's closet to listen to what he had to say."

"I thought you and Bess wanted me to let Drew handle it?" I accused, unable to resist the same sort of jab he'd made at me earlier.

"I know," he said, a little sheepish. "I'm sorry. But in my defense, the police were there when I was eavesdropping."

I smiled. "It's okay. I was curious, too. Did Drew ask you where you were on Wednesday?"

"Yes?" Eli admitted. "I saw her standing at her door at different times throughout the day. But I never did talk to her that day. He asked me something else that I didn't hear him ask Gil."

My eyebrows shot up in surprise.

"What?" I asked.

"He asked if I had ever been to Flinch, Texas?" Eli told me. "He wanted to know where I was on March 15 twelve years ago."

I was stunned for several moments. My brother asked Eli if he was in Flinch the day Ruby Doyle disappeared.

"He asked Bo about it, too," Eli confided.

"What'd he say?" I asked, unable to contain my curiosity.

"Twelve years ago, Bo was a coach at Crosbytown," Eli explained what he'd heard. "It's in the next county over from Flinch. It was Bo's first year to teach...and he coached track."

I gasped. "So he could have known Beth back then? He knew Leigh was really Beth?"

Eli shook his head. "I don't think so. Drew only called her Leigh, and Bo only referred to her as Leigh. Later, Drew asked him about Beth and Ruby Doyle. Bo said of course he remembered it because it had been all over the news then."

"So he was dating Leigh here, but he had no idea she was Beth Doyle?' I tried to get my facts straight.

"That's how it sounded to me."

My mind was on overload by this point. Gil was Beth Doyle's cousin. So did he know that whoever took Ruby was supposed to be here? And Bo was dating her, but he didn't know she was really Beth?

They both seemed upset that she was gone. And I didn't want to believe that either one of these people could actually kill anyone. I'd known both of them all my life, and no matter how I felt about Bo, I hoped it wasn't either one of them. But if it wasn't Bo or Gil, then who else was out there that had any kind of a reason to kill her?

CHAPTER 17

I tried my best to work after I left Eli's room, but it was hard to concentrate on anything.

Why was it that at the exact time I finally realized how I truly felt about Eli and how he really felt about me, a killer happened to be in town? That was a selfish thought, but my brain was all over the place at that point, and I still had to go home and clean my room that had been plundered.

When Eli popped into my room at four o'clock, I shut my computer off and told him I'd meet him at my Jeep. I turned to close the blinds and caught sight of the poetry book again. I decided to take the cards home now so that I wouldn't forget them. I had decided, at some point during the day, to put them in an old scrapbook I had at home so that I could keep them.

I put the cards in my purse and locked my door on the way out. The lights were already out in the hallways. Normally, I wouldn't have paid the dimness any attention, but with all that had happened, I found myself walking faster than normal.

Just as I rounded the corner to the main hallway, I slammed into something and fell flat on my rear.

Startled, I looked up to see Mr. Scott standing there.

"Ms. Kelley?" the principal said, extending his hand.

I blushed, greatly relieved that the lights were off. The afternoon light spilling in the windows and glass doors provided enough light to see by, but the corners and recessed doors along the hall were shrouded in the shadows.

"Thank you, sir," I said, taking his hand. "I'm sorry I ran into you."

"Quite alright," he assured me. He helped me up off the floor, and his hand lingered on mine just a second too long.

My whole body went cold, and I turned my attention to picking up my purse. I had my purse in hand when Mr. Scott handed me the bright pink note card I had received from Leigh.

"Thank you," I said, taking the card and putting it back in my purse.

He nodded and smiled. He hardly ever smiled, but that was the second time that day that he had. He was a courteous man and a good principal, but he rarely ever smiled.

I shook my head to dispel the thoughts. I was just overwhelmed by the stress and situations and revelations of the last two days.

"Eli's waiting on me," I told him. "See you Monday morning."

"Monday," he said, stepped around me, and walked off the way I had just come from.

I had just stepped away from where I'd fallen when I saw a slight movement through an open door. I stopped in my tracks. The door was open a crack, but I caught a glimpse of an eye and an ear, and then the door slammed shut.

My heart hit record speed, and I got out of there fast!

Darby wanted to spend the night with Noelle again, so I let her. At the moment, I felt more comfortable with her there than at our house, and I still had to clean up my room, anyway. I didn't want her to see that.

Eli walked me in the house this time. He checked the house while I waited in the kitchen. All was clear.

When he came back to the kitchen, I was lost in thought, staring out the window across his yard. His hand on my elbow brought me back to the present just in time for me to realize his other hand was now cupping my cheek.

I lost my breath as I looked up at him. It was true that I had finally begun to realize the feelings we were having for each other, but I had never seen Eli Bloom look at me the way he was looking at me just then. And our mutual admission of wanting to be more than friends earlier that day wasn't helping me any either.

He pulled me even closer and tilted my head back a little. I thought my heart was going to break through my rib cage. He smiled a little wickedly when a sigh escaped me, and he leaned his face closer to mine.

Over an agonizingly slow number of seconds, his lips moved across my cheek to stop at my ear.

"Do you know how hard it is not to kiss you right now?" he whispered.

I tried to speak, but words failed me.

His cheek was hot against mine, and I couldn't concentrate. Somehow, my hands found his waist, and I could feel the muscles under his shirt.

I closed my eyes and ran my hands around his waist and up his back. It was my turn to grin as he sighed in my ear. We were both on the verge of losing our senses.

"Quinn." His lips moved against my ear.

I smiled at the movement, at the sound of Eli whispering my name.

Miraculously, I found my voice, somewhat anyway.

"We're...torturing each other," I whispered back.

"I know," he said, taking a deep breath. His hands moved then. He wrapped me in a bear hug, a gesture I was used to from him.

I rested my head on his chest and said, "I'm gonna talk to Carter tonight. He'll be here soon."

"Good," Eli said, kissing the top of my head. "The sooner, the better."

I chuckled softly against his chest, and he laughed with me, stroking my hair.

Suddenly, the side door banged open. Mattias, Carter's best friend, was through the door first, and he stopped short when he saw Eli hugging me. We didn't jerk apart, but Eli gave me an affectionate squeeze then let go just as Carter walked in.

Carter smiled. "Hey, Unc."

Mattias was still standing there a little dumbfounded. Fortunately, Carter didn't think anything of it; he saw Eli hug me all the time.

"Carter." Eli beamed a brilliant smile. "You and Mattias are going to take care of your mom tonight, right?"

"Yes, sir," the boys said in unison.

"Do a good job," Eli told them, playfully. "I'm just a few feet away if you need anything."

"Thanks, Unc," Carter said with a smile, nudging Mattias to head up to his room.

When their backs were to us, Eli planted a kiss on my cheek. He was turning to go when we heard Mattias, who was obviously trying to whisper, but failing at it miserably, say, "Man, they look like they need a cold shower."

My face turned red as a beet. I could feel it. But Eli only chuckled beside me, then he left for home.

CHAPTER 18

As soon as Eli left, I locked the door and got up to my room to clean it. I wanted to get it over with. Nothing was missing, not even my computer. Either I surprised them just about as soon as they came in or they had an idea of just what they were looking for.

I wish I knew what they were looking for.

I was convinced that the break-in had to do with Leigh Taylor's death, but what did they think I could possibly have?

I had invited Leigh over to supper back in the fall, right after school started. She was new then, and I wanted her to feel welcome. She came to eat a few times, but by Thanksgiving, she was always busy when I asked her. I still saw her at church, and we had lunch every now and then in town, but she never came over to eat again.

Leigh must have been preoccupied with finding the man who took her sister. That and apparently she and Bo had become an item. But it was beyond me how they kept it under wraps in a town like Sutter. Everybody knew everybody else's business.

But we only had Bo's word to say they were together; we certainly couldn't ask Leigh. Of course, there was no telling what my brother might turn up about them in his investigation, but I doubted he was going to fill me in.

Maybe Bo was lying about how he felt about Leigh to cover up something horrible he'd done. Then again, maybe he wasn't. He certainly seemed to be very truthful when he'd spilled the beans to me earlier. And no matter how I felt about the man, Leigh could have loved him. Besides, he just didn't strike me as a killer. Arrogant, yes, but a killer? I highly doubted it.

What do I know, anyway? I thought to myself, exasperated. Bo or Gil or any number of people could have poisoned Leigh and broken into my house right under my nose, and I wouldn't have known it because, apparently, I was so oblivious that I couldn't even tell that my best friend was in love with me! Nor could I realize that I was in love with him until a sweet woman dropped dead, forcing me to look to him for comfort and normality and safety.

I smacked myself in the forehead so hard it stung.

Why hadn't I seen it sooner? It took about a year after John died for me to be okay to be alone, to be able to rest through the night, to not look out the window every time I heard a car because I thought it was him. Sure, there would always be a sound or a word or a place that would bring John to my mind, but I wasn't the lost mess I had been in those long months after he died.

The passing of time helped my heart heal. Prayer upon prayer for peace and comfort were finally answered, and I had finally been able to do more than exist.

Then a revelation hit me like a Mac truck.

The Lord works in His own time, I heard clear as a bell. It was so clear, in fact, that I turned around to make sure I was alone. But I was still by myself in my now clean room.

I couldn't hold back the smile that erupted on my face.

I walked over to the window and glanced up at the beautiful evening sky. The sun was going down, and off to the west thin, white clouds shown against a backdrop of orange and pink and blue.

"Yes, sir," I said to the beauty above. "Thanks for reminding me."

A few minutes later, as I showered in my own bathroom, I heard a tap on the door. It was Carter saying that he and Mattias had ordered pizzas for supper, which was a great relief right then because I didn't want to cook. So after my shower and shrugging into some comfy clothes, I laid down a minute to rest.

The last few days had been hectic, and I was bushed.

As soon as my head hit the pillow, I drifted off. A few seconds after that, I was sitting on my front porch swing. A light breeze fluttered across my face, and John was sitting on the porch step.

Immediately, I felt a pang of guilt at having been so wrapped up in Eli earlier. But as soon as the guilt hit me, I realized I was only dreaming and John was really gone.

I hadn't dreamt about John in so long that I didn't want to move. I just wanted to look at him for a little while. He was still just as handsome as the last time I'd seen him alive—his dark hair was still wavy and a little shaggy, and his blue eyes matched the sky.

He smiled, and my heart lurched.

Then he was sitting next to me on the swing. Tears stung my eyes, and I looked up at him.

"John," I whispered.

His smile became softer, and he reached out and touched my cheek.

I could feel his hand! I could *feel* it!

But I didn't dare move. I'd never been this close to John in a dream before; he had never been this clear in my mind.

His eyes flitted across my face to look over my shoulder for a second, and then he was gazing into my eyes again.

"Be happy," he whispered as I looked up at him.

"John—" Tears clouded my eyes and my throat ached. I blinked several times to clear my vision and—

He was gone.

I slumped in the swing, and it swayed with the movement. I just wanted to wake up now that John was gone, but something pulled at my attention.

I looked over my shoulder, in the direction John had just looked.

Eli waved at me from his porch, and I woke up.

CHAPTER 19

Carter and Mattias cleaned up the kitchen after supper, and I went to sit out on the porch swing. Unlike my dream, it was dark outside. The stars shone brightly, and it was nice and quiet out on the porch.

I was gently swinging in the porch swing when Carter came out to check on me.

"You okay, Mom?" he asked, plunking himself down beside me and propping his arm behind my shoulders on the back of the swing.

I smiled and looked up at him, but I had to look away after only a moment. He looked so much like his dad it hurt right then.

"I'm the mom," I said quickly, trying to cover up my inability to look him in the face. "I'm supposed to ask if you're okay."

He laughed and squeezed my shoulder.

"Then ask me," he prodded.

The grin crept across my face, unbidden. Of course, he was going to make me feel better.

"Are you okay?" I asked, able to look at him again.

"Yes, ma'am." His smile beamed brilliantly. "Now, are you okay?"

"Yes," I sighed, catching a glimpse of Eli's house over Carter's shoulder.

I needed to talk to Carter about Eli.

"He's home," Carter said, catching my line of vision. "I'm sure he'd like a goodnight kiss."

My mouth dropped open, and I sat up straight as a board.

"Carter Aron Kelley!" I cried in shock. "What? Why, why would you?"

"Don't get hysterical, Mom," he said, patting my shoulder as he stifled a laugh. "Just a kiss, though. You'll have to behave until you get married."

"Carter!" I exclaimed, slapping his chest this time.

He couldn't stifle any more of his laughter as he squeezed me into a ferocious hug. It didn't take but a few seconds for my shock to be replaced by relief.

Carter knew how we felt, and he wasn't even phased by it.

"How did you know?" I asked, still holding onto him.

"I just did," he answered. "It's kind of obvious."

"How?" I demanded, pulling back to look at him. "How is it obvious? Bess said the same thing. It wasn't obvious to me."

"Really? It wasn't?" he asked, skeptical.

"No. It wasn't," I assured him. "It just…kind of hit me suddenly." I paused a second. "And now, it's like…it's familiar. Sort of like, we've always felt this way."

"Maybe you have," Carter suggested.

I was taken aback at that, especially coming from him.

"Carter, I loved your father with all my heart," I assured him. "I always will. I was not—"

"Mama," he said to silence me, "that's not what I meant."

I shook my head slightly, confused by this conversation.

"I meant you two have always been friends," he explained. "You've loved him since before you met Dad, because people love their friends. The kind of love just changed, but it was always there."

The wheels turned in my head, and it became clear. Yes, I had always loved Eli. It just took all these years, and all that had happened to us, for my love to morph into the romantic love I felt for him now.

I smiled at my wonderful son, shaking my head.

"Since when did you get so…wise?" I asked, leaning against his shoulder and staring out into the night sky. "You haven't even finished ninth grade yet, and you can read me like a book."

He laughed. "I'm sorry, have we met? I am the offspring of the brilliant John Kelley."

I slapped his leg at his pretended arrogance, and we continued to swing in silence, staring at the stars.

CHAPTER 20

Carter and I eventually had to go back in. Poor Mattias was alone in the living room watching a movie.

When he saw us, he jumped up, and he and Carter checked all the doors and windows. All was secure, so we trouped upstairs. I said goodnight to the boys and went to my room.

The clock on my bedside table read 9:45 p.m. I thought it was later than that, but apparently not.

Darby had already called when we were eating, so I didn't have to call her again to check on her. I just sent Beth a quick text to say goodnight and got ready for bed.

I was looking forward to sleeping late after the crazy week we had all just had.

Wouldn't you know it? The phone rang at seven thirty the next morning. So much for sleeping late!

I groped around on the bedside table without opening my eyes, finally finding my phone.

"This better be important," I groaned into the phone.

"Excuse me, young lady," a stern familiar voice came through the phone, "I taught my daughter better manners than to answer the phone in such a rude way."

"Mama," I gasped, my eyes popped open wide, and I sat up straight in the bed. "I'm sorry. I—"

Her soft laughter cut me off.

"It's okay, sweetheart," she assured me. "I figured the mad-mama voice would wake you up."

I smiled and sank back into the pillows.

"Yes, ma'am."

"So why haven't you called me?" she asked, a little worry creeping into her voice.

"I'm sorry," I apologized. "I didn't want to ruin your trip or worry you. We're all safe and sound."

"I know you are, baby," she told me. "But I would have liked to hear it from you."

"Yes, ma'am," I said again. "When are you coming home?"

"Depends on your father," she said, sounding a little exasperated. "I'd like to head home today, but you know how he is when he gets fascinated by something."

I laughed, remembering my childhood. We couldn't afford big vacations, but my daddy would take us all out camping or fishing or on spontaneous road trips. It was wonderful, like a big adventure. He'd tell us stories and keep us entertained for hours. But, Lord help us if anything ever distracted him. An odd road sign, a historical marker, a weird bug—it didn't matter—if he was fascinated with it we were stuck until his curiosity was satisfied. Then, and only then, could we move on. I couldn't give him too hard of a time about it, though. All those back roads and stories and long rides in the car looking at old buildings helped mold me into a history buff and, later, a history teacher.

"Don't worry about it, Mama," I told her. "Enjoy your time away."

"Yes, well..." her voice trailed off. "Are you sure you're okay? Carter and Darby, are they alright?"

"Yes, ma'am," I assured her. "We weren't home when the guy broke in. The kids were at their friends' houses. Eli came over immediately to help me, and he called Drew. Nothing was missing."

"Drew told me all of that," she admitted, "and it worried me. They picked the perfect time to break in, and they left valuable property behind. It wasn't a random robbery, sweetie."

I sighed. "I know," I told her. "But don't worry, we'll figure it out."

"How about you let Drew figure it out," she advised. "He's got the badge and the gun."

"Yes, ma'am."

I wasn't going to argue with her. I didn't want her to worry. I didn't have any intentions of sticking my nose in if I could help it. Although, I doubted that I *could* help it. I just hoped I didn't see any more eyes staring at me from dark rooms or find any more prowlers in my home.

I went back to sleep after my mom's call, but I was wide awake by eight forty-five, so I got up and showered. After brushing my teeth and getting dressed, I was just putting my hair into a ponytail when the phone rang again.

The touchscreen of my phone read ELI. I smiled and answered, a little more courteously than I had with my mother.

"Morning, beautiful," Eli said.

I blushed even though I was alone in my room.

"Good morning," I said back, and then I had to tell him about Carter.

"You know," I said, "my son suggested I come over and give you a goodnight kiss last night."

There was silence for a moment.

"I knew I liked that kid," he said after a second of silence.

I chuckled and rolled my eyes at him, even though he was at his house across the yard.

"Smart-aleck," I teased. "But seriously…Carter said it was obvious how we felt. He was…happy about it."

"Happy is good," Eli said, and I could hear his smile through the phone. "Let me know what Darby says. I'd like to take you on a date next Saturday."

A date?

I hadn't been on a date in years!

"I'm going to talk to her when she gets home from Bess's," I told him. "It's my objective for the day."

I heard his soft chuckle and my heart flip-flopped.

"Awesome," he said. "I'm going out to my brother's today, but I wanted to make sure Carter was going to be around. I don't like the thought of you alone anymore."

"He'll be here," I said. "Sticking close to home today."

"Okay," he said. "I'll call you when I get back this afternoon."

"You better," I told him. I wanted to be able to walk over to his house and fall into his arms right then. It had taken me this long to figure out what was right in front of me, and I didn't want to waste any more time. But I had to talk to Darby first. I had to at least broach the subject of Eli with her before I stumbled any farther.

Eli was about to hang up, when I stopped him.

"What?" he asked, startled.

"A thought just hit me," I said, remembering back to the library yesterday. "Drew questioned you and Gil and Bo."

"Yeah."

"Do you know who all they questioned?"

"Well, Gil left with Drew to go back to the sheriff's office," Eli said, confirming what I already knew. But what he said next came as a surprise. "But later I saw Jess coming out of the library. Zindt had questioned some people."

My heart sank. Of course, they would question him. He was out in that area twelve years ago finishing up his last semester of college; that was where he met Donna. But there was no way in creation that Jess had anything to do with all this. I was hoping for some other person for my brother to look into—I just wasn't sure that suspecting murder out of Bo or Gil was barking up the right tree.

"Jess told me who went in after him," Eli confessed.

"Who?" My curiosity perked up.

"Reeve Scott."

CHAPTER 21

Later, as I loaded laundry into the washer, I thought about what Eli had told me. Drew had questioned Bo and Eli and Gil. Then, Zindt took over after Drew left and questioned Jess and Mr. Scott.

Immediately, my bump into Mr. Scott yesterday after work flooded my mind. He was hired as principal the year before Jess became assistant principal, so he'd been at the school for four years. He had always seemed a little distant, but he was always courteous and professional. I had never thought anything about him as strange, until yesterday when he helped me up after I stumbled into him.

It was only a second, but his fingers had lingered on my hand; I had to stoop to get my purse just so I could pull my hand away without seeming rude. But a moment of awkward contact didn't make him a killer.

And who was that looking at us from a darkened room? I knew that room—it was Ms. Widlow's room; she'd taught Geometry in that room for the last twenty-eight years. We all had her class in school, we all knew her, and there was no way that was her looking at us.

Ms. Widlow was only five feet tall, and the person I'd seen was a good deal taller. Who would be in her room? Were they looking at me or Mr. Scott or both of us?

I sighed, exasperated, putting the lid down on the washing machine and heading for the kitchen. I plopped down in a chair at the table.

I was beyond frustrated. I wished there was some way I could help, but I just didn't know what was going on. And I didn't want to stick my nose in and draw more attention to myself than I already had. I didn't want this mystery man to come back; he might catch us at home if he did, and then where would we be?

Good thing Drew is the sheriff, I thought, *and not me.*

Then in the next second, I was wondering how I could usually figure out the bad guys in the mysteries that I often read, but presented with it in real life, I was stumped.

That figures!

Thundering footfalls down the stairs brought me back to reality. Carter and Mattias appeared, ready to raid the kitchen for lunch. They pulled out the leftover pizza from the night before and whatever else they could find to consume.

Teenage boys are always hungry and will eat just about anything.

The side door in the kitchen opened then, and Darby walked in.

"Hey, girl," I said with a smile, "long time, no see."

She came straight to me and kissed me on the cheek. Then the refrigerator door shut, and she could see Mattias standing there. She blushed, and Carter and I both had to look away to hide our grins.

Darby had turned ten back in January, and ever since, she had decided that Mattias was the most handsome boy she'd ever seen. I don't know what turning ten had to do with boys, but it was like flipping on a light switch for her. She announced to Carter and I that Mattias was wonderful and that she was going to marry him someday.

"Hey, Little Bit," Mattias beamed at her as he set food down on the table.

"Hi," she said grinning from ear to ear.

I figured I better remove her from Mattias's immediate presence before she melted, so I shooed her upstairs, to leave the boys in peace.

I needed to talk to her, anyway, and I figured catching her in a lovey-dovey mood was as good a time as any. Once in her room, she dove onto her bed and rolled over on her back. She sighed, still grinning.

"Mattias is so handsome," she told me. "Isn't he, Mama?"

I laughed and plopped down beside her.

"Yes, baby," I agreed. "He is a very handsome young man. But you are too young to worrying about boys."

She shot me a skeptical look.

"I'm not worrying, Mama," she assured me. "And I won't always be ten. One day, I'll grow up and become Mrs. Mattias Shore."

I sighed, shaking my head, but I still couldn't stifle my smile. Anything was possible.

"Well, since we're on the subject of boys, I want to discuss something with you," I eased into the subject of Eli.

She looked horrified for a second.

"Is this 'the talk'?" she questioned, using air quotes to emphasize "the talk.'" "Noelle said Aunt Bess gave her 'the talk,' and it was gross."

I really couldn't hold the laughter back then.

"Well, sweetheart," I began, "if 'the talk' is gross, then you need to keep your mind off boys for a while."

She seemed to contemplate the thought for a moment. Then the shock and awe wore away.

"It'll be alright one day," she assured me. "We can't get married until I'm eighteen, anyway."

I just shook my head again. There was no way around the matter of Mattias right now, so I turned back to what I needed to say.

"I was talking about me," I told her. "I...like someone. I like them an awful lot, and I wanted to talk to you about it."

"You're asking me for advice about boys?" she asked, shocked, but grinning.

I chuckled again.

"Well," I said, "kind of. I want to know how you feel about it."

"Is he nice?" she questioned.

Eli's sweet ways ran through my mind.

"Very nice," I assured her.

"Do you like him the way I like Mattias?"

I thought that one over. How could I compare adult emotions to a ten-year-old's crush? But I had to admit that some of the feelings probably weren't that different.

"Yes," I told her. "He's wonderful, and I could definitely see a future with him."

"Does he like kids?"

"He already adores you and Carter," I assured her.

"He does?" she perked up.

"Yes." I smiled. "And you like him, too."

It took her a second, but realization finally washed over her.

"Uncle Eli!" she squealed.

She seemed happy, and happy was good.

"Yes, baby," I admitted. "You think that would be okay? For me and Uncle Eli to start seeing each other?"

"Did you tell Carter?" she questioned.

"Actually, he told me," I confessed. "He said he could tell how Uncle Eli and I felt about each other."

She continued to stare at the ceiling. It was decorated with a dozen different butterflies that John had hand-drawn and painted for her when I was pregnant with her. I knew she was thinking of her daddy, then. She had seven short years with him, and then he was gone.

What was swirling around in her head? I wondered.

What came out of her mouth was totally unexpected.

"I don't wear pink," she told me, matter-of-factly. "So if there's a wedding in this future you're planning, I get to pick out my own dress. Deal?"

My mouth dropped open, but I soon recovered.

"Deal," I said.

We shook on it and hugged. I couldn't even explain my relief at that moment—both my kiddos were happy! But, then again, I don't know what I had been so worried about. Eli was already a part of our lives, so it wasn't a big leap for us to include him more so.

Just then, my phone rang.

I kissed Darby on the head and headed to my room where I'd left my phone earlier. The number was a phone number I didn't recognize. Usually, I wouldn't answer numbers I didn't know, but it tugged at my curiosity for some reason.

I pushed the button to answer and put it to my ear.

"Hello?" I said into the phone.

There was silence for a minute. I was about to say hello again when I was cut off.

"Where is it?" a voice demanded.

"What?" I asked confused.

"Where is it?" the voice asked again.

"What is *it*? Who is this?"

"I know she gave it to you," the voice insisted.

She? My heart jumped into my throat.

Leigh!

"I don't have anything," I assured him. The voice was definitely a man, I decided, but I couldn't recognize it.

A short, harsh laugh rasped through the phone.

"Yes, you do," he assured me, "and I will do anything to get it back."

I gasped, and the phone went dead.

CHAPTER 22

I wasted no time in dialing my brother's number, and I was waiting for him on the front porch when he pulled into my driveway a few minutes later. The lights on his truck were flashing, but no siren sounded. I handed over the phone as soon as he walked up.

He checked the number and wrote it down in his notepad. He let me keep my phone, though.

"Drew, I don't have anything," I insisted, before he could ask any questions.

I had already explained to him what all the voice had said earlier.

"Are you sure?" he asked. "Nothing at all?"

"What could I have?" I exclaimed.

"I'm not sure," he said. "But I think you do have something."

"Drew!" I cried out. "I'm not lying! I don't—"

He put his hand on my shoulder, hoping to quiet me.

"What I mean, Quinn, is that I think you have something but don't realize it," he explained.

"What? How? Wh—"

"I sent the deputies back to Leigh Taylor's house today," Drew said. "Her father showed up yesterday while I was questioning Gil Pargo. Turns out, he is Leigh Taylor's cousin. I took him to the station yesterday. They both gave me some info that made us go back to Ms. Taylor's to have another look around. They also said some things that make me think you have something."

I didn't mention I knew Leigh was Gil's cousin, and I threw my hands up in exasperation and dropped into the porch swing. What in the world was I supposed to have?

Drew sat down beside me. "Gil told us about a safety deposit box. He gave us the key. Leigh asked him to keep it for her."

"What was in it?" I asked, beyond curious.

"Mostly newspaper clippings and maps," he said. "We're combing through those now. There was also info on several men at the school. The girl did her homework. But she never pinpointed who she actually thought it was that took her sister." He paused for a second. "There was a short list in there, too."

"A list of what?" I prodded.

"Not much," he admitted. "But enough to make me believe you have something."

"Spit it out, Drew," I snapped at him. "What did it say?"

"Ruby was in love with an older man," he began. "Ruby is dead. The Whispering Widow holds all the clues."

I nearly fell off the swing from shock.

The Whispering Widow. My gaze trailed out across my yard to the road sign at the corner.

WHISPERING LANE

I was the widow who lived on Whispering Lane. If I hadn't been sitting down, I think I would have fallen down.

"Quinn," Drew said as I sat there in shock, "Leigh called her dad on Tuesday. She told him she had figured Ruby's disappearance out, and she asked him to trust in the Whispering Widow's help."

I squeezed my eyes shut and covered my face with my hands. Why did Leigh think I held all the clues?

"Did she say anything to you? Did she come over? Did she ever give you a gift?" Drew fired questions at me.

Concentrate! I told myself. *Think!*

"She came over for supper back in the back in the fall a few times," I said. "But she hasn't been back here since—"

My voice dropped off, and I jumped up. Drew stood up beside me.

"I let her borrow a book," I blurted out and ran into the house.

Drew's footsteps pounded behind me through the door and up the stairs. I was first in my room, and I quickly scanned my bookshelf. I pulled the old paperback off the shelf and handed it to my brother.

"She borrowed this?" he confirmed.

"Yes," I told him. "She brought it back last week, the Friday before she died. I sent her up here to put it back because she said she wanted to borrow another book."

"So she was up here by herself."

I nodded. "For a few minutes, yes."

Drew looked at the book and quickly flipped it open.

A note card fell out.

We exchanged a confused glance as Drew stooped to pick it up by the corner. He looked at it closely, and his eyes popped round as saucers.

"Read this, Quinn." He turned the card around carefully, still holding it by the corner.

It was Leigh's careful, neat handwriting.

It read:

> It wasn't a game, Quinn. It was my insurance policy. I'm glad I met you.
> I know you can figure it out!
>
> Leigh

"What wasn't a game?" Drew questioned me.

"The poetry!" I gasped.

"What poetry?"

"The lines of poetry," I said, heading for my purse. "It was a guessing game that Leigh and I played. We both love poetry, so she made up a game out of putting lines on note cards in my box. I had to guess which poem it was. If I got it right on my first guess, she had to buy me a Dr. Pepper."

I pulled the cards out of my purse.

"Lay them out on your bed," he said, laying the book and note card he had on the bed. He got out his cell phone and called the sheriff's office.

"Zindt," Drew said into the phone, "you and Pitt get over to my sister's house. Now. Bring a camera."

I laid them out in order. Each one had the date written, small, in the top left-hand corner. Each card was a little different. There was a bright green one with the verse in purple marker, a few white ones with all the letters of the words in different colors, an orange one with heart stickers on three corners, the bright yellow one with glitter glue, and the hot pink one.

"You know all these poems?" he asked.

"Yes, of course," I told him. "I guessed most of them right on the first try. Except for the line, 'I found a thing to do...'"

"What poem is that?" he asked, leaning closer and looking at the yellow card.

"Porphyria's Lover," I answered.

"The note said Ruby loved an older man," Drew said. "That a love poem?"

I made a face thinking back to the poem. "Not love like you're thinking," I told him.

His eyebrows raised, curious.

"Then what is it?" he asked, slowly.

"It's about a man who wants his lover to adore him," I explained. "Then, when he realizes that she does adore him, he wants to keep it that way always, so..."

My voice trailed off, and Drew looked worried.

"So...what?" he asked, his posture stiffening for the bad news.

"So he strangles her with her own hair so he can have her to himself, forever."

CHAPTER 23

"Oh, my Lord!" Drew exclaimed, throwing his hands in the air. He started pacing a short trail back and forth in front of the door. "I'm assigning Zindt to watch your house. When they get here, I'll have Pitt take pictures so you can try to help us figure out these clues. I'll have to take the originals back to the station."

I was staring at the cards, my mind already going over the lines and the poems they came from. I barely heard what Drew said as he paced back and forth. It only took a few minutes before there was a knock at the front door. Drew was gone down the stairs and back again with Zindt and Pitt and the camera.

"Pitt, take several shots of all these cards—fronts and backs—and then print out a set for Quinn," Drew ordered. "She's going to help us try to figure out these clues."

"She is?" Zindt asked.

"Yes," Drew said, "she is."

"But, sir," Pitt interjected, "what if something goes awry and word gets out that a civilian was working on this—"

I finally looked up then, tearing my attention from the cards. Drew didn't look happy, and Zindt and Pitt looked like they were wishing they had kept their mouths shut.

"Zindt? Pitt?"

"Sir?" they asked in unison.

"Either one of you read much poetry?" Drew asked, a little sharply.

"No, sir," Zindt said first, and then Pitt said the same.

"Well, Quinn does," he told them. "She's familiar with all these poems, and, apparently, Ms. Taylor wrote these lines down in particular because she had faith Quinn could figure it out."

They kept quiet and looked sheepish.

"Now," Drew went on, "are we going to have a problem here?"

"No, sir," they both answered again.

"Good." Drew pointed to the note cards. "Pitt, get those pictures taken and printed ASAP."

The camera started clicking.

"Quinn," Drew said, turning to me, "we need to look around more. We won't make a mess. Can you get the kids out of the house for a bit?"

I nodded. "Sure."

I left the three of them in my room to go make some calls and get the kids squared away.

Thirty minutes later, the kids were gone, and Zindt and Drew were searching the house. Pitt was putting each card in an evidence bag while I looked over the freshly printed pictures of the note cards. Something caught my eye on the backs of the note cards, but in the picture, I could barely see it.

"Pitt, stop," I said, walking over to the bed. "There's writing on the back of the note cards, but I think it's in pencil; I can barely read it."

"Yes, ma'am," he said, helping me look at the backs of the cards. "They say who...what...why...how...and where."

I thought of Leigh, then. Why'd she have to be so mysterious? I would have helped her. All she had to do was tell me what was going on.

"I wish I'd seen this earlier," I said, mostly to myself. "Maybe she'd still be here if somebody knew she was in trouble."

"Maybe," Pitt said. "But now you do see it, and you can help her."

"You weren't too keen on me helping a few minutes ago," I pointed out.

"I was just noting a possibility," Pitt explained. "It wasn't anything against you personally."

"Ah," I said, absently. "Well, I hope you're right, about helping her, I mean."

"Me too."

Drew and Zindt didn't find anything that didn't belong in the house. Most likely, all I actually had were these note cards and the clues they held. Pitt left to go back to the station with the originals.

Suddenly, as I stared at the pictures just as Zindt and Drew were finishing their search, the front door banged open.

"Quinn!"

I jerked at the sudden noise. That was Eli.

I forgot to tell him the cops were here!

"Quinn!"

"She's fine, Eli." I heard Drew shout from across the hall.

I dropped the pictures on my desk and ran to the top of the stairs. Eli shot up them in a flash, wrapping his arms around me. I wrapped my own arms around his neck in return, and he lifted me up, my feet leaving the ground.

I couldn't help but smile against his neck. He smelled like fresh-cut grass. It was the sweetest scent I could think of at the moment.

As my feet settled back on the floor, I left a light kiss on his neck, right under his jaw. He was shocked, but he grinned at me as he straightened up.

"I'm standing right here," Drew groaned, drawing our attention to Darby's doorway where he was standing with his hands on his hips.

I covered my grin with one hand, but Eli stood straighter and cleared his throat.

"Sorry, Drew," Eli apologized. "I saw your truck and a deputy's car outside. I was worried."

Drew looked like he didn't know what to think. I was glad Zindt was still downstairs for the awkward moment.

"Are you two—?" Drew's voice trailed away as he gestured at us.

Eli looked down at me, grabbing my hand. His smile was wonderful.

"Are we?" he asked me.

I know my face went a little red because my brother was standing there. But I was still glad to be standing there, getting to admit to someone that Eli and I were together.

"Yes," I said.

When we looked back to Drew, his expression hadn't changed much. He walked right up to us, getting nose to nose, almost literally, with Eli. They were roughly the same height as each other, easily about 6'3".

"You better have good intentions, Bloom," Drew warned. "You're my buddy and all, but if you ever hurt my sister or my niece and nephew, well, I'm just gonna have to shoot you."

"Drew, I—" Eli started, but I shoved Drew, cutting Eli off, because my brother was barely holding back his laughter.

"Stop it," I told Drew, then leaned closer to Eli and his hand I was holding. "Don't worry, Eli. He told John the same thing."

Drew finally cracked a smile. He stuck out his hand, and Eli shook it.

"I am kidding," Drew assured him. "But only because I know you're a good guy. So stay that way."

"I will, I assure you," Eli promised, then his face turned serious. "So what is going on? Why are y'all here today?"

Drew and I filled him in, taking turns speaking. Eli's grip on my hand tightened as we explained.

"Zindt's going to be stationed outside for a while," Drew said. "Pitt will switch out with him every twelve hours. The guy flat-out threatened you on the phone. I'm not taking any chances."

"I understand," I said. The knowledge that Zindt was going to be right outside my house twelve hours a day finally hit me. Not that he was just tripping all over himself to go out with me, but he had asked me out several times. I didn't want him to get any ideas now that he'd be around, especially not since Eli and I were an item.

"I have to get back to the station," Drew said. "I need to look through the pile of stuff from Taylor's safety deposit box."

I gave Drew a hug and thanked him for coming over. He smiled and then headed off downstairs.

Eli turned to me as soon as Drew was on the staircase, and wrapped his arms around me, a slow grin crawling across his face. I grinned back, but a blush was creeping up my neck.

"Behave, Bloom!" Drew shouted from downstairs. "Remember, I still have a gun!"

I laughed and buried my face in Eli's chest, extremely grateful that I was now able to hold onto him.

CHAPTER 24

I gave Eli a shy kiss on the cheek and then pulled him downstairs. I had to call John's mother because my kids were with her. I called and told her I'd be over there within the hour to pick them up.

Eli was standing so close as I hung up the phone that I thought I'd lose my senses. I nearly dropped my phone trying to put it on the counter.

He smiled at my nervousness and moved closer. All the breath left my lungs.

"You're so beautiful when you're flustered," he whispered, smiling softly, putting his hands on my hips and pulling me toward him.

"I am?" I breathed out, not even truly realizing what he'd just said.

"Oh, yes," he whispered.

I buried my face in his chest again, blushing, unable to keep looking at him. One of his hands came up to stroke my hair.

"What's wrong?" he asked, his chin resting on top of my head.

"Nothing," I assured him, wrapping my arms around his waist. "Nothing. I'm just..."

"Just what?" he asked.

"A little embarrassed," I admitted.

"Embarrassed?" he asked, sounding skeptical. "About what? Aren't you the same person who was kissing my neck a few minutes ago?"

"Shut up?" I said against his chest, slapping his back with one of my hands as they were still wrapped around him. "It comes and goes. You'll have to learn to live with it."

"If it involves you," he told me, "I can learn to live with anything."

Zindt knocked on the door asking to use the restroom while Eli was still holding me in the kitchen. We stifled groans of aggravation, and I planted another peck under his jaw just to mess with him. This time, he returned the gesture, and I was tempted to leave Zindt on the porch as my neck tingled where Eli had just kissed me.

But I let Zindt in, and then Eli and I went to get Carter and Darby from their grandmother's after Zindt had gone back outside. When we got back, I told Eli I needed to look at the note cards from Leigh and that I'd call him later.

I barely made it two steps from the front door when I heard a knock at the side door.

It was Eli.

"What are you doing?" I asked with a grin. "I told you, I'd call you later."

"I know," he said, leaning closer. "I just wanted to tell you something."

"What?"

"Don't wait too long to call me," he whispered, and then he put his cheek to mine so he could talk directly in my ear. "I know we kind of just decided this thing, but I've been thinking about us for a long time."

"And?" I murmured, a little confused, but still loving the fact that his cheek was touching mine.

"And I've been waiting a long time to kiss you," he said. "I also think that a first kiss out under the stars would be wonderful."

I closed my eyes, reveling in the thought of kissing Eli.

"You're killing me," I whispered as he pulled back to go.

"What do you think you do to me?" he asked, winking at me. "Call me...soon."

"I will," I promised and then forced myself to get back to those note cards.

I decided to work backward with the note cards. The last one was the hot pink card. It said WHERE on the back. The verse read,

"ROUND ABOUT THE PROW SHE WROTE." A prow was the front of a boat. In "The Lady of Shallot," the lady writes her name on the prow as she's dying, so the people will know who she is when the boat floats down river to Camelot.

This card was the last one Leigh gave me, so I figured she was trying to tell me where something was around here. But I didn't know what that something might be.

Maybe it was the name of the killer. Maybe it was some evidence.

I called my brother before I lost my train of thought.

"Figure this out?" he asked, hopeful.

"Not exactly," I told him. "But I think something is hidden on the front of a boat."

"A boat?" he questioned.

"Yes," I told him and then read the line out loud. "'ROUND ABOUT THE PROW SHE WROTE.' The lady in the poem wanted the people to know who she was. Maybe Leigh put the name of the killer or some evidence on a boat. The people she had info on, the people you questioned, check them out to see who has a boat."

"Already on it, sis," he said, most agreeably. "Any time, day or night, call me if anything hits you."

"I will," I promised.

"Gotta go," he said.

"Hey, Drew," I said quickly before he could hang up.

"Hmmm?" he grunted into the phone.

"Don't razz Eli too hard, okay?"

I could hear his smile through the phone. "Now what kind of big brother would I be if I didn't harass your boyfriends?"

"A nice one," I told him. "At least keep your gun in your holster until I get my first kiss in!"

There was a chuckle, and then the phone clicked in my ear.

Big brothers could be a pain, even when they're all grown up.

A migraine thwarted our starlit rendezvous later. Darby got them without warning sometimes. But she'd been at Bess's for two days, and she'd probably played her heart out. Most likely, she was just overexerted, and the migraine came as a result.

Eli was understanding, as he always had been in the past. I promised a rain check on the kiss under the stars, and he offered to take Carter to church the next morning if Darby was still feeling poorly.

The next morning, Darby was still ailing, so Carter went to church with Eli. Eli gave me a peck on the cheek at the side door as Carter barreled through the kitchen. As soon as they left, I locked the door and headed for the stairs.

Across the street, I could see Zindt's unmarked vehicle parked in the shade out through the living room windows. He wasn't in his car, though. But as I rounded the corner of the kitchen to go back upstairs, I caught sight of him through the window in the back door. He was dressed in jeans and a collared shirt, no uniform.

He saw me and waved, so I waved back. I also quickly retreated up the stairs. My phone started to ring as I reached the top of the stairs. I made a mad dash to answer it because I had left it in Darby's room when I went to answer the door for Eli. I pushed the answer button before I picked it up so it would stop sounding and not disturb Darby, who had just managed to go back to sleep.

I didn't even get out hello before a voice said, "They can't help you."

It was the man from yesterday.

"What?" I gasped.

"The police," he said. "They can't help you. They didn't help Ms. Taylor, and they won't help you."

I eased out of Darby's room and shut the door quietly.

"Who are you?" I demanded.

A harsh chuckle.

"Wouldn't you like to know," he said. "All you need to know is that I am very close, so you better give me what I'm looking for. Or, next time, even your precious Mr. Bloom won't be able to help you."

Click.

The line went dead.

CHAPTER 25

"Zindt!" I exclaimed from the porch a few seconds later. His window was rolled down, and he heard me, immediately hopping out and coming over to the porch.

"Ma'am?" he asked, concerned.

"That man called again," I told him. "Call Drew."

"Yes, ma'am."

I stepped back to pull the door closed, but he caught it with his hand. The move startled me for a second.

"I need to wait with you," he insisted.

I started to protest, but I figured it was procedure. I let go of the door and walked back inside with Zindt close behind. He called Drew as I made my way to the kitchen table and sat down.

Zindt asked me what the man said after hanging up with my brother, so I told him. He made notes on his notepad. I got up then and fixed both of us a glass of iced tea while we waited on Drew.

"Zindt, I need to ask you something," I said as I handed him a glass of tea and sat back down.

The hint of a smile played at the corners of his mouth. For the moment, I ignored it. I knew he liked me, and I was hoping those feelings for me would work in my favor for a few minutes. I wasn't going to play up to him, but I wasn't going to discourage him either.

"Ma'am," he asked.

"You cannot ask me how I know this," I warned him.

His smile formed at the thought of us sharing a secret. He nodded slightly.

This question had just occurred to me again. I hadn't really registered any thoughts about it since Jess had told us. But now, it seemed even more important.

"I know Leigh Taylor called your office a few days before she died," I told him.

His smile faltered a little, but not entirely.

"There wasn't much to it," he assured me, twisting his iced tea glass in a circle on the tabletop.

"Well, she's dead, Zindt," I said, flatly. "Maybe there was something to it."

"I took the call myself," he said, defensively.

"So what did she say?" I asked, perking up a little in my chair.

"Ms. Kelley, I don't know if I should—"

"Please, Zindt," I said, instinctively reaching out and laying a hand on his wrist. "Drew has asked me to help. I'm in this now."

His eyes dropped to my hand, then, and I realized what I had done. While all I knew of Zindt told me he was a competent deputy and a nice man, I also knew full well he would take any form of contact between us as an indicator of affection.

"I'm sorry," I said the first thing that popped into my mind and withdrew my hand.

"It's quite alright," he assured me, still smiling.

"The phone call, Zindt," I urged. "What did she say?"

He looked around as if someone might hear.

"She only asked for Sheriff Darby," he told me. "She wouldn't leave a message. But he was out of town. He didn't get back until after she was dead."

I nodded. Yes, the call itself may have sounded like nothing. But the fact that she only wanted to talk to Drew wasn't just *nothing*.

"She just asked for Drew?" I questioned. "That was it?"

He nodded. "She asked for Sheriff Darby. She refused to leave a message, and she wouldn't talk to anyone else."

If she knew something solid, why didn't she just tell a deputy? But if I thought about it, the woman had devoted her life to finding this man because the police never had. She must have wanted to talk to someone in charge to ensure things would be done right this time.

Drew came through the front door then. He questioned me and Zindt about the call.

"I checked the number out yesterday," Drew told both of us after we answered his questions. "It's a prepaid cell phone, so that's a dead end."

"I haven't really looked at the note cards again since I called you last night," I confessed. "Darby's sick."

Drew nodded. "Back to your post, Zindt. I need to talk to Quinn."

"Yes, sir," he said, and then he was gone.

"I drove around some this morning," Drew told me, "just to see who had boats. Bo Blalock has a boat, so does your principal, Reeve Scott, and Jess Carwright."

"Jess?" I questioned. "Leigh wouldn't put something on Jess's boat!"

"Oh, really?" he questioned, skeptical.

"Drew!" I exclaimed. "Jess Cartwright is one of our best friends. We have literally known him since birth! He does not—"

"Quinn! Zip it!" he snapped, stopping me. "I simply said he has a boat. If she was trying to hide something on a boat, his boat would be as good as any."

I let out an audible sigh of relief. My heart returned to a normal beat.

"Do you have any idea what it might be?" Drew asked. "This something you think that she hid."

I thought about it for a moment. If it was a thing, it had to pertain to her sister. Or maybe she stashed the name of the killer since she had left this trail of bread crumbs without specifically pointing the finger at anyone.

I stared off toward the wall behind Drew's head as I thought. There were four pictures there all arranged around a fifth. In the center picture frame were me, John, Carter, and Darby sitting under a shade tree—Carter was five and Darby was just a baby. The pictures surrounding the center were taken the same day. Darby lay in a basket surrounded by flowers, her blue eyes shining in one frame. Carter sat on a rock by a lake, his elbows on his knees, his chin in his hands, his smile beaming in the next frame.

Under the center frame was Carter and Darby laying on a red-and-white checked tablecloth surrounded by green grass as they both smiled up to the camera above them. The last frame was John and I. His dark hair was wavy and just a little shaggy, as usual, his blue eyes shone brightly behind his round silver-rimmed glasses, and he held me close. The top of my head just reached his shoulder, and I leaned into him, smiling just as he was.

I'd seen those pictures every day for years, but something in one of them pulled my mind back to another picture I'd seen recently. Something round and silver.

I sprang to my feet and pulled at Drew's arm as I dashed by him. He nearly toppled over trying to get out of his chair. I let go and he followed me.

"What is it?" Drew demanded, stopping behind me in my room.

Before I answered him, I shot Bess a quick text, labeling it an emergency. Then I sat down at my desk and booted up my computer.

"Quinn?" Drew asked, again.

"I remembered something from the day I got the letter," I told him. "Give me a sec."

He stood behind me, shifting from foot to foot as I searched again for one of my recent searches.

"There." I pointed to the screen when I found what I was looking for.

"It's an article about Ruby Doyle," he said, leaning in.

"Yes," I said. "But I mean that…right there."

He followed my finger to a specific line.

"Ruby Doyle also wore a silver pendant the day she disappeared," he read aloud.

"It was never found," I assured him, because I had read about that, too. "What if Leigh found it? After all these years, if Ruby Doyle was killed, there's nothing left of her. Except maybe if the man who took her kept something."

"And if she did find it," Drew continued, adding a few cars to my train of thought, "she'd want to keep it safe. It'd probably be the only link to what happened to her sister and to who this killer is."

"I texted Bess," I told him. "She has an old picture of Donna at a track meet. Ruby Doyle is in it wearing the necklace. We were looking at it the night I gave you the letter."

He straightened up again.

"I need to talk to her dad and Gil again, see if they have any pictures of it, or can describe anything unique about it."

He reached out and ruffled my hair, then. I slapped at his hand—he knew I hated it when he mussed my hair.

"Thanks, sis," he said, with a grin. "You're about to put me out of a job."

"Oh, no," I assured him. "I'm naturally curious, and she asked for my help. By the grace of God, I've hopefully figured out a few things."

"Well, your ideas sound good to me," he told me. "Gotta go. Zindt's outside. Call you later."

He left, and I checked on Darby. She was still sleeping, so I decided to take a look at those note cards again.

CHAPTER 26

Eli brought barbecue for lunch after church. I saw him walk out to Zindt's car and hand him a bag before he came in the house. Carter, Eli, and I ate at the table; Darby was still in bed.

"You want some help looking over those note cards?" Eli asked, when we were finished eating, the kitchen table was cleaned up, and Carter had retreated upstairs.

I let out a sarcastic, "ha!" before I realized it. He looked truly hurt for about three seconds, and then his grin appeared again.

"You can help if you want," I told him, by way of apology, but then I pointed out, "I just didn't figure a math guy for poetry."

He rolled his eyes and then stood up, slowly. My pulse quickened as a mischievous grin spread across my face. He took my hand in his and knelt down in front of me as I sat at the table, stunned into silence.

"Shall I quote for you, my dear?" he asked, playfully.

"Nah," I teased. "Poetry might be a little beyond you."

He feigned insult and clutched his chest. Then, he smiled again.

"How do I love thee? Let me count the ways..." he began and then proceeded to recite, quite perfectly, the rest of "Sonnet 43" by Elizabeth Barrett Browning.

By the time he finished, I truly was stunned. And I was no longer grinning.

Eli stood up and pulled me along with him as he spoke. His arms slipped around my waist, and I stared up at him in awe of what I was hearing. It was wonderful.

Right at that moment, when he finished the poem, I didn't want to have to wait around for a starlit night. He had created a beautiful moment, right there in the kitchen, on a bright Sunday afternoon.

Eli felt it, too. His eyes searched my face as the seconds ticked away on the clock on the wall.

Suddenly and slowly all at the same time, his hands left my waist to cup my face. He tilted my head back just a little more and leaned in.

My eyes closed instinctively, my heart hammering against my chest. I felt like a silly girl about to be kissed for the first time ever.

Then...

Then there was a knock at the door.

We froze.

My eyes flew open to see Eli and inch from my face. He didn't look too happy to be disturbed.

He kissed my cheek quickly, let go, and headed for the door. I flopped back down in the chair.

"Your bladder is extremely punctual, Deputy Zindt," I heard Eli grouch a few seconds later.

I had to cover my mouth to stifle my laughter.

Eli's mom called while Zindt was in the restroom.

"To be continued," he promised, squeezing me into a hug as he was about to head out to check on his mom.

"You're on," I promised back, closing the door behind him. I watched him walk out to his truck and then turned to go back upstairs.

I walked right into Zindt's chest. I stumbled, and he held my arm to steady me.

How long had he been standing there? I wondered silently. His fingers trailed down my arm as he let go.

I stiffened, and a chill ran up my spine.

He was smiling.

"Pitt will be here soon," he told me.

He was standing close enough that I wanted to back away, but the closed door was behind me.

"Alright," I said, trying to ease around him. "I need to check on Darby."

He sidestepped slightly, blocking my way. Immediately, I wanted to slap my brother for letting this guy be one of the officers watching after us. I wasn't necessarily afraid of him, but he was intimidating. He wasn't quite as tall as Drew and Eli, but it was clearly obvious that he was regular at the gym. His broad shoulders and muscled arms looked perfectly capable of dispatching the bad guys without even having to use his gun, but what if he got perturbed with one of us?

"Are you and Bloom an item?" He was smiling, but he still looked a little odd somehow.

"Yes," I said, quickly. Maybe a little too quickly.

"Okay, sorry to be nosy," he said, moving out of the way.

He went around me without another word and went back outside to his car. I stared after him for a second.

Zindt was one strange cookie. With as persistent as he had been on occasion when he had asked me out before, it surprised me that he just walked off after I simply answered yes to his question.

Was I wrong about him? Maybe I was reading more into his smiles and gestures than there really had been.

Too much was running rampant in my mind these days. I just shook my head and got back upstairs to take another look at those note cards.

CHAPTER 27

I combed through the poems for the next few hours. I already had a book of poetry in my room that contained most of the full poems, so I put tabs on the pages to make them easier to find.

Then I went to the bed and sat cross-legged on it with the pictures laid out in front of me and the book of poetry in my lap. I thought about what Drew said: Ruby loved an older man.

The orange card with the hearts stuck out at me. I picked up the picture, and reread the line:

> I love thee to the depth and breadth and height
> My soul can reach...

Oh, how well did I know that poem? I thought. Eli had just quoted it to me earlier that day. The back of the orange card read "HOW."

I looked away out the window, thinking, still holding the picture in my hand. The poem was most definitely about love. And Leigh said this all had to do with the man who took, and/or killed, her sister. Her sister was in love with an older man.

How? I looked at the picture of the back of the orange card again.

Maybe that was just simply how it all started—love. Possibly, an all-consuming love, which would make sense if you took into account the line from "Porphyria's Lover."

I looked to the picture of the yellow card and its back view. The back said, "WHY."

The man in "Porphyria's Lover" is deranged. He contemplates how to keep his love with him forever. He decided to kill her, thinking he is fulfilling her wish to always be with him. But truly, he's just obsessed and believes the only way to have her just as he wants her is to kill her.

A shudder I wasn't anticipating went through me. This person, whoever he was, had been obsessed to the point of murder with Ruby Doyle. Maybe he was just like the man in the poem, in that the girl loved him, but he had to control the outcome. Maybe she wanted to end it, and he snapped. There was no way to know if he actually strangled her, but I believed Leigh, this man hadn't just taken Ruby; he murdered Ruby.

I pulled myself away from the cards for a moment to check on Darby. She was awake, but resting, so I made her a bowl of chicken noodle soup and sat with her for a while. The medicine she took for her migraines often wiped her out for about a day, so she'd probably lay around until time for school on Monday.

After I had her tucked away again, I deposited her bowl and spoon in the sink and went to the fridge for some tea. Carter's baseball schedule was on my refrigerator door, and it brought Bo Blalock to mind.

I thought about Bo as I trotted back up to my room, my glass of sweet tea in hand. I wanted to think Bo hadn't done this, but what if I was wrong? Just because I'd known him all my life didn't mean he was innocent, but it didn't mean he was guilty either.

Unfortunately, these thoughts brought another person to mind—Jess. I was immediately swamped with guilt for even thinking it, but I had to admit that he was in the area when Ruby disappeared. Donna, his future wife, was watching Ruby run track the day she disappeared. Donna actually knew Beth and Ruby.

"No!" I said suddenly, and very loudly, to myself. The sound echoed in the room, and I covered my face, exasperated.

"Lord, forgive me," I whispered, quite near tears.

How could I even think that of Jess? Even if I didn't say it out loud, how dare I think it? Jess and Eli and Bess were my best friends!

But what did I have that would point to Bo as a murderer? Still...

I couldn't get Bo out of my head, so I called my brother again.

CHAPTER 28

"Pitt is on his way to relieve Zindt," Drew said into the phone as soon as he knew it was me on the other end. "What's up? Figure out anything?"

"I wish." I sighed. "No one knew that Bo was dating Leigh, and no one knew Gil and Leigh were cousins until she died, and that just seems a little sketchy to me. You're the cop. Do you honestly think that either one of them is capable of committing murder twice?"

He sighed into the phone. "Anything is possible. Anybody can be pushed into anything, given the right circumstances."

I was quiet a minute. "I knew you'd say something like that."

"Trust me, sis, we're looking at every possibility," he assured me. "I know you don't want it to be Bo or Gil or anybody else we know, and neither do I, but the sad fact is that we do know this person, even though we haven't figured it out yet. They're close...so any ideas would be helpful right now."

"I have a few," I confessed, not wanting to admit part of it.

"Well?" he prodded.

"The first part is obvious," I told him. "How and why...Ruby fell in love with a man who became obsessed and killed her."

"What's the second part?" he questioned.

I sighed, not wanting to open my mouth. We already had this possibility in mind, but I had hoped after his confession to me that it wasn't really going to be him.

"Quinn?"

"Leigh was involved with Bo," I said. "I know she didn't broadcast it, but I know she wouldn't just casually date someone. From my friendship with her, and from what we're figuring out about her, I believe if she was with someone, it'd have to be serious...or intentional."

"Oh," he said into the phone, and I could practically hear the wheels turning in his head.

"She could have been in love with him, or...she had figured out the culprit was Bo, so she started dating him intentionally."

"If he figured out who she was, he would eventually have to find a way to keep her quiet," Drew surmised.

"I know we haven't really seen eye to eye with Bo in nearly twenty years," I told my brother, "but I hope it's not him.

"Me, too, sis," Drew agreed. "Me too."

I didn't sleep well Sunday night. I didn't get to see Eli for the rest of the day; he was at his mom's late helping with a plumbing issue. A few texts were all we managed the rest of the evening.

At about 1:00 a.m., I got up and went downstairs for some warm milk. I nearly jumped out of my skin when I saw a figure walking across the front yard, but it was only Pitt making his rounds. I decided to make him some coffee since he was having to stay up. He was grateful a little while later when I got it out to him.

Later, after my milk and Pitt's coffee, I finally dozed back off. But I dreamed of running through the halls at school and finding Ms. Taylor over and over again. By the time the dreams subsided, I only had an hour or so to sleep.

By the time we all made it to school, I was already exhausted. I hugged Eli at his door and walked across the hall to mine and unlocked the door. The rest of the morning, until my conference fourth period, I walked around in a fog.

My mind kept running lines of poetry like it was a roll of film. Sir Lancelot kept riding down to Camelot, and a crazy man sat in a cabin with a dead woman's head leaning on his shoulder. I tried to shake the thoughts away and concentrate on my lessons, but it was a losing battle.

I was relieved when fourth period rolled around. I gathered a small stack of papers and headed upstairs to make copies.

Gil was there. But I didn't know what to say. Nobody was supposed to know Eli and I had eavesdropped on his interview.

He looked up when I walked in. I wondered how he would react to me seeing as how my brother had escorted him off to the police station for questioning just the week before.

When he smiled, I wondered if he recognized me for a second.

"Hi, Quinn," he said, waiting on his copies to finish.

"Hi."

"I think Drew finally believes me," he told me.

"Believes you?" I asked.

"Yes, uh…" he began. "Leigh Taylor was my cousin. Well, Beth Doyle was, Leigh wasn't her real name. But you know that last part, right?"

"Yes," I admitted. "Drew asked me to help out with a few things."

I didn't know how much he knew that I knew about the case.

He nodded. "He came by yesterday asking about Ruby's necklace. I suppose you know about her, too."

I sighed. "I do. I got a letter in the mail from Leigh the day she died. It just said she was really Beth Doyle, and that she was here because of her sister's disappearance. There was an article in the envelope about Ruby."

"I figured as much," he said, shaking his head and turning back to the copier.

"What do you mean?" I asked.

"Nothing," he said, removing the copies and setting the next pages to copy. He looked sad all of a sudden.

"Gil, what is it?" I prodded, taking a step closer. "Is it important? Did you tell Drew?"

He sighed. "Yes. I practically had to tell your brother my life history, even though he knows most of it. I grew up on the same street as you two. You'd think he'd know I couldn't do this."

"I'm sorry, Gil," I told him. "Drew has to do his job."

"I know," he assured me. "I'm just complaining. Bad mood, that's all. Beth and Ruby were great people. It hurts that both of them are gone now."

I was at a loss for words. I didn't want to keep saying I'm sorry. I was sorry, but repeating it wasn't going to help anything.

"Gil, can I pray for you?" I asked.

He was quiet a moment. I didn't know where he stood spiritually, but he used to come to church with us when we were kids, so he was used to being prayed for.

"Sure," he said, quietly.

He didn't look up. His hands were planted on the copy machine even though the machine was done and quiet.

I sat my papers down and put one hand on his left arm and one hand on his back. He turned his head away slightly, but not before I caught sight of his misty eyes.

I asked the Lord to watch over Gil's family and to give them peace in such a terrible, confusing situation. I asked God to heal their hearts and save their souls and protect them throughout their days. I also prayed for them to have the strength of the Lord to persevere through these hard times.

"In Jesus name, amen." I finished, but I didn't let go of his arm or move my hand from his back.

"Look at me, Gil," I said, softly.

He did, and his eyes were pink behind his glasses.

"We know that whatever we do won't bring them back," I told him, honestly. "But I know Drew and I know me. We won't let this go. I promise you that."

He smiled, shyly. It was a smile from the sweet kid I knew from down the street, so I smiled back.

I dropped my hands, and he wrapped me in an unexpected hug.

"You were her friend," he said, pulling back. "She told me so. And you've been my friend when you could have brushed me to the side. Thank you."

"You're welcome, Gil," I said, sincerely.

He let go and gathered his stuff. He turned to go but turned right back around.

"She was getting paranoid," he said, flatly.

"What?" I was confused.

"Leigh, Beth," he told me. "I knew why she was here, of course. But every year that passed, she was getting more obsessed, more paranoid. She wouldn't even trust me with what she found. She gave me that safety deposit box key the day before she died, and I think she only did that out of desperation."

I thought about that for a minute. That was why she would only speak to Drew. It was why she left clues in poetry and hid whatever it was that she found.

"Thanks, Gil," I told him. "We'll find him."

CHAPTER 29

I managed to muddle through the rest of the day. Eating lunch with Eli was a bright spot, but the afternoon was much like the morning.

John's mother called to say she'd pick up Darby from school, which was fortunate because I had papers to grade. Eli said he had a stack of papers to go through, too, so he retreated to his room.

I was halfway through my stack when my phone rang again.

It was that number!

I looked around in a panic.

I don't have anything! I wanted to yell at him.

But instead, I stopped the incessant ringing by pushing the answer button.

My first attempt at hello didn't come out, so I cleared my throat.

"Hello," I said, calmly.

"This is a test," he told me.

"A test?"

"Yes."

"I'm hanging up," I told him. "Whatever it is you want, I don't have it."

"That's not why I called this time," he assured me. "Do not hang up."

A pause. Silence.

"Do not tell the police I called," he said. "And believe me, I will know if you do. This is your test."

Click. Nothing.

I was tempted to throw my phone across the room, but I didn't want to break it. I turned and looked out the window. I needed to figure out which boat she left this clue in.

It had to be the necklace. What else could he want? Gil said she was paranoid these days. If she wanted it to be safe until I found it, then I doubted she'd put it on the killer's boat. She put it somewhere she thought it would be safe. Somewhere she knew I would find it.

Maybe she did put it on Jess's boat, I thought. She knew we were all friends. If it wasn't there, though, I couldn't think of another place a paranoid woman would consider safe.

The door shut behind me abruptly, and I spun around quickly in my desk chair.

"Bo!" I stood up quickly, bumping my chair, and it went rolling back toward the wall.

He made a beeline toward me, and I was glad the desk was between us from the look on his face.

"This witch hunt you and your brother have out for me is outrageous!"

He wasn't out and out shouting, but he wasn't quiet either.

"Bo—"

"Shut up, Quinn," he snapped. "Yes, once upon a time, I was a stupid kid. But I already told you what happened that night, and you said you believed me."

"Bo—" I tried again.

"I loved Leigh," he insisted, his face contorting into a pained look. "It wasn't a fling. Drew came to my house yesterday and questioned me again. He even dug through my boat looking for God only knows what."

"Bo!" I snapped this time. "It's not a witch hunt. Drew is looking at everyone who could possibly have anything to do with all this."

"Yeah," Bo snapped back, sarcastically. "But I bet he's looking at me just a little bit harder than everyone else."

"As hard as this may be for you to believe," I told him, trying to stop his tirade. "I want you to be innocent. No matter what happened with me when we were in high school, I do not want you to be guilty of this. Neither of us does. I've known you all of my life, Bo. I hope and pray that you are innocent."

He stopped and stared blankly. A little steam had gone out of his sails.

I knew full well that I could be wrong, but I just did not want Bo to be guilty of this.

He was quiet when he spoke again. "I am innocent. I don't need to pray about that. I pray you and Drew get over this grudge against me and find out who really did this."

Then he turned and left just as abruptly as he had entered.

No sooner had Bo gone than Eli came in. He must have just missed Bo. Jess came in right on his heels. They closed the door behind them.

"What is it?" I asked, my chest tightening at the look on their faces.

"Drew and Alvarez just went in Scott's office," Jess said. "They told me to leave the front office."

I thought about telling them about the phone call; they weren't police after all. But I kept my mouth shut. Instead, I mentioned Jess's boat.

"Jess, I'm helping Drew with this case," I told him and then filled him in on the poetry. "She hid something on a boat. She would have hidden it where she thought it would be safe. Can we look on your boat...now?"

"If it'll help," he told me. "Go for it."

We tore Jess's boat apart, which probably wasn't a good idea, after we thought about it. Drew would have preferred that he and his officers go through it, but I couldn't wait.

I wanted to find what we were looking for, what the mystery man was looking for. I wanted him to be caught and locked away. I wanted this mess to be over.

I wanted justice for Ruby and Leigh.

But I also had selfish reasons running through me. I felt guilty about it, but I was having a hard time trying to keep my mind off Eli. I loved him, that's all there was to it. There was no denying the fact. But I did feel bad catching my mind wandering to him when I needed to concentrate all my senses on figuring out these clues left by Leigh.

As we helped Jess put his boat back in order after not finding a thing besides some of Chantry's long-lost army men, I thought about just how stumped I was.

"It wasn't Gil or Bo," I blurted out suddenly, and both Jess and Eli straightened up, temporarily forgetting their task of putting everything back.

They looked at each other and then at me.

"How do you know?" Eli asked, a little skeptical.

"I don't know," I said, frustrated. I kicked at a clod of dirt next to the boat trailer. "Bo's already confided in me twice now. He looks distraught over losing someone he loved, not guilty of murder. And Gil's her family—"

"He is?" Jess asked, shocked.

We hadn't told anybody what we'd overheard yet.

"Yes," I confirmed, "and I saw him earlier in the copy room. I even prayed with him. He was upset, and he told me that Leigh was getting paranoid. Paranoia would explain her leaving hints in poetry and hiding evidence rather than going to the police."

"True," Jess said. "But what does her being paranoid have to do with Gil being innocent?"

"It doesn't," I said, despondent. "But I just don't think he did it. I don't think either one of them did."

Jess and Eli looked at each other again and then back at me.

"Then who does that leave us with?" Eli questioned.

"Well, it can't be Jess," I said, wanting to put it in words that I did not think it was him, one of the closest friends I ever had.

Jess gasped, hurt. "Me? Seriously?"

"No!" I cried, going over to him and grabbing his arm. "I trust you like I trust Eli and Bess. I could never think something so terrible of you. I sincerely meant it can't be you. So that should only leave us with one feasible possibility."

It hit them quickly and at the same time.

"Reeve Scott," they said in unison.

CHAPTER 30

We decided to drive over to the sheriff's office from Jess's house. I called to check on Darby, and she was having fun in the garden with John's mom. Carter texted me to say he caught a ride to Bess's to help Coye with a horse, so my kids were preoccupied for at least a few hours.

Rasher met us at the front desk.

"Can we see Drew?" I asked him.

"Let me check," he told us, winding his way through the office of desks and filing cabinets and around a corner out of sight.

Eli slipped his arm around my waist and pulled me to him while Rasher was gone, kissing me on the top of my head. Jess was standing behind us and half-giggled, half-cleared his throat. We both turned to look at him, but where Eli was grinning, I was a little embarrassed.

"I didn't say anything," he said, throwing his hands up as if in surrender, grinning to himself.

"You don't have to," I scolded. "Let me guess. It was obvious to you, too."

He shrugged, never losing his grin, looking off at an imaginary wall. I rolled my eyes, not really aggravated but truly baffled at how everyone knew but me.

"Well…" he said, finally looking back at us, "only since about the seventh grade."

I gasped. "Jess, I had a husband, you know."

"Yes, and he was my friend, too," Jess assured me, his features softening at the mention of John. "But you two." He gestured back and forth between us. "I predicted that years ago."

Rasher walked back up, then, before I could form a response.

"Y'all can go on back," he said, pulling back the swing gate that separated the public reception area from the office.

We trouped one behind the other through the office, around the corner, and into Drew's office. Jess shut the door behind us.

Drew looked up from the mass of papers on his desk.

"What is it?" he asked, his eyes going from one to the next. "Something happen?"

"Nothing in particular," I said as we all sat down. "I just wanted to fess up to going through Jess's boat. We didn't find anything."

"Quinn—" he started, none too happy.

"Don't read us the riot act," I said, holding up a hand. I thought about the call earlier but didn't say anything. He was sure to call back, and then I'd tell Drew. "I know it's the necklace. It has to be. So I knew what we were looking for. Did you get a better description?"

He sighed, shook his head, and rummaged through the stack in front of him.

"Better than that," he said. "Mr. Doyle had a picture."

Drew pulled a picture from the stack. It was a close-up of Ruby Doyle and another girl who much resembled Ruby.

"Beth?" I asked, pointing to the other girl.

Drew nodded. "Or Leigh Taylor, as we know her."

Eli leaned over my shoulder. "She looks, looked, a little different," he observed. "Not just getting older, different."

Drew nodded. "Dr. Doyle said she had a nose job done in college to repair a deviated septum. That changed her looks a little, but the rest was superficial. While she was here, she kept her hair a very dark brown, and she wore blue contacts. The coroner already told me about the contacts. Her dad told me about her. She was really a blond, like her sister, and her eyes were green."

"So the killer was probably surprised to find out she was here," Jess pointed out. "She came here last summer. She's had lots of time to dig up dirt."

Drew nodded. "And dig did she ever," he said, gesturing to the papers in front of him.

There were manila file folders fanned out on his desk. Some were fat, some were thin. A stack of maps lay to the right and a stack of newspaper clippings to the left.

I ignored the mass of paperwork for a moment and looked back to the picture. Ruby's silver pendant was as big around as a fifty-cent piece, at least. There were swirls expertly etched into the silver and a square sapphire in the middle of the pendant.

"Did Dr. Doyle say where she got it?" I asked, looking back up to Drew.

Drew nodded but didn't speak.

"C'mon Drew," I prodded. "Where'd she get it?"

He sighed. "Where do you think, little sis?"

"The older man?" I asked.

"Her father knew?" Eli piped up, shocked.

"And he didn't mind?" Jess inquired.

"What is this? The third degree?" Drew cried.

"Well?" I insisted.

"He knew it was from her boyfriend, but he never met the boyfriend," Drew explained. "I looked back over interviews I got from the Kingston County sheriff's department. They just got here this morning. Apparently, the boyfriend was a big mystery. None of her friends had ever met him, not even her sister."

"So how did Leigh dig all this up?" I asked, confused. "Gil said she's been at it for years. How'd she know where to look? Who to suspect? Who to *not* suspect?"

"Well, I don't think she did at first," Drew explained. "She wondered. She pestered the police from the time it happened until she got out of college. It'd be my guess that she kept notes and articles on everything. Then she put her journalistic skills to good use."

"Journalism?" Eli asked.

"Yes, her degree was in journalism, not English," he told us. "Beth Doyle was a journalist for a few newspapers before taking a teacher certification test four years ago, right after changing her name to Leigh Taylor. And then there's the internet. You can find just about anything about anybody as long as you can Google."

We all nodded in agreement.

"Have you got any pertinent info out of all this?" Eli asked, pointing at the stacks on Drew's desk.

Drew sighed heavily, leaning back in his chair and contemplating the stacks before him. "Somewhat," he told us.

"Somewhat?" Jess exclaimed. "Out of all that, all you have is somewhat?"

"Well, I know you're innocent," he said, looking directly at Jess. Jess went pale. "What?"

"She had a file on every male above the age of thirty at the school," Drew told us, pulling a thin file out of the stack. "This is you, Jess." He opened it and began to read aloud, "Jess Alex Cartwright, age thirty-three, birthdate March 2, blah, blah, blah. Here's your daily routine at school, where you went after school—"

"What?" Jess exclaimed, getting up and leaning over the file. Drew lay the file out flat so that we could all see it.

"I told you, Jess, she was a reporter," Drew reminded us. "She researched all of y'all. Took pictures. Followed you."

"Stalking?" Eli asked in disbelief.

"Well, yes," Drew said. "But she only wanted information, so to my knowledge, she never approached anyone or made harassing phone calls. Did she ever bother either of you?"

"No," Eli and Jess answered together.

"That's what I figured," Drew said, nodding. "I'm fairly certain she managed to get all this info without ever being noticed—"

"Until she took that necklace," I interjected. "She found it, Drew, then tried to call you. Somewhere in there she hid it, probably waiting to talk to you."

He thought about that a minute. "Makes sense," he said. "I've still got to keep digging through all of this." Drew gestured around at his desk. "Jess's file is straightforward. Along about the end of September, she concluded that he was innocent—"

"And you didn't?" Jess snapped. Jess rarely ever gets angry, but when he does, he tends to explode. I scooted my chair closer to Eli.

Drew was being professional. "I just became aware of these files a few days ago, but, yes, I had concluded your innocence," Drew said, firmly. "But what kind of cop would I be if I didn't look at everyone objectively? I am looking into every possibility, but you're my friend, so I looked into you first. Twelve years ago, when Ruby Doyle disappeared, you were home for a few days. Your dad broke his leg, remember?"

Drew paused briefly and Jess nodded, visibly cooling off, settling back into his chair. I breathed a sigh of relief. I was surprised he didn't get mad at me earlier, but he'd taken it all in stride until just a few seconds before.

"So I knew you couldn't have taken Ruby. Therefore, you wouldn't have any reason to kill her sister," Drew continued. "Then we got this...pile. The last page says, 'Cleared it wasn't him'."

"Oh," Jess said, at a loss for any other response.

Drew sighed again. "Look, Jess," he said. "Don't be angry. I have to look into every feasible angle."

"I know," Jess nodded. "Really, I do. I'm just...kind of floored. I've never been considered for murder before."

"What about me?" Eli asked, before anyone could another word.

"Cleared," Drew said, "by me and by her. Actually, she cleared you pretty quickly, according to her notes. You were never over in that area like Jess had been."

"Good," Eli said.

Drew smiled then and looked at me.

"She did make a few interesting comments about your boyfriend here," Drew said, leaning on his elbows on the desk. Then he straightened up and grabbed another thin file. "Elijah Dixon Bloom, personal info, blah, blah, blah," Drew jabbered.

For some reason, I knew I was about to blush.

"August 31. Eli Bloom is the right age but was never in the area of Flinch," Drew read aloud. "Glad it's not him. He's a real gentleman. I wonder when Quinn Kelley is going to put the poor guy out of his misery. LOL."

I covered my face, but Eli just patted my back as Jess stifled laughter with a fake cough.

"Even complete strangers knew," I complained into my own hands. "I am not that dense."

"It's okay, sis," Drew told me. "We're just giving you a hard time."

I dropped my hands and tried to look exasperated, which wasn't too hard at the moment.

"Drew, you said 'somewhat' earlier," Eli reminded him, crossing over into the serious stuff again. "All of the files aren't like ours?"

"Mostly, they are," he told us. "But Blalock and Pargo's files are mostly written in some code. Who knows what it all means. And at least one is missing."

"Missing?" I asked. "How do you know that?"

"They're numbered," he said, flipping Eli's folder closed and pointing to a red number "3" on it. "And in alphabetical order. Mr. White is the last number. If there's another number after him, I have no idea. I have Anders, Blalock, Bloom, Cartwright, Donner, Gunnerson, Moss, Pargo, and White. It's just as I said, every man over thirty. Since they're in alphabetical order, guess which one's missing?"

Oh, Lord, I thought. I could still feel his hand lingering on mine.

"Mr. Scott," I guessed what I knew to be true.

Drew nodded. "Mr. Reeve Scott, Sutter High principal and, once upon a time, Junior High Social Studies teacher at—"

He dropped off, letting us guess for ourselves.

"Flinch Junior High?" I guessed again.

"As I said earlier, little sister," Drew went on, "keep making good guesses, and I'll be out of a job."

CHAPTER 31

"Can you arrest him?" I asked, hopeful.

Drew sighed and looked away for a moment.

"Knowing she kept a file on all of these men, and that his is missing does look...suspicious," he told us, looking back at us. "But, no, I can't arrest him."

"What? Why not?" I exclaimed.

"Arrest him for what? I don't have any solid proof," Drew said, firmly. "Alvarez and I went to the school and questioned him again. I've reviewed the notes from when Ruby disappeared. All of her former teachers were questioned. The Flinch school is small, and the junior high and high school are on the same campus. All those teachers were questioned and checked out. Mr. Scott, in particular, was at a workshop that day."

"But why would his file be missing?" I asked, gesturing to the manila folders. "And what did he say on Wednesday? Y'all questioned us then."

"Zindt talked to him," Drew explained, rummaging through another pile and pulling out another file. He flipped it open, looking over the info there. "He was in the office most of the day. He evaluated Mr. Moss right before lunch. He spent both lunches in the cafeteria. Sixth period, right after second lunch, he was back in the office. He was on the phone when Mattias came running in the office."

I thought for a minute. "Was she poisoned? For sure?" I asked, just realizing that I hadn't found out if that was a definite.

Drew nodded. "The county medical examiner said yes."

"Then he could have done it," I suggested. "Mr. Moss's room is just past ours. He could have slipped something in her cup on his way to Moss or back out on his way to lunch."

"So could you," Drew pointed out. "You told Pitt you saw her getting coffee right before sixth period."

"Drew—" I began, but he cut me off.

"Quinn," he said, quietly, "the plain fact is that she was poisoned from a cup that any number of people passed by and had access to—"

"But—"

"But nothing." Drew put an end to my side of the argument. "Until Alvarez and I questioned him today, he didn't even know Leigh Taylor was Beth Doyle."

"Or so he says," I pointed out, but my brother shot me a look that wasn't pleasant.

"I won't throw speculation around, Quinn," Drew stated, matter-of-factly. "I won't ruin someone's life on a hunch. I want y'all to be safe, that's why Zindt and Pitt are watching y'all. But I can't in good conscience arrest a man who has an alibi for the previous case and who seems to be answering all my questions truthfully now."

I started to open my mouth again, but Eli laid a hand on my arm, so I clamped my mouth shut. This arguing was getting us nowhere anyway.

"Look, baby sister," Drew continued, "I know what I'm doing, and I never said I trusted the man. We'll get this figured out. In the meantime, I'd really appreciate you looking over those poems some more."

"Yes, I need to," I acknowledged. Just because I was convinced I'd figured out part of the clues, the necklace in particular, didn't mean I had it all figured out. I needed to get back to them.

"Well, I've got work to do," he said, eyeing the articles and files. "I'll call you later, Quinn. See her home safely, fellas."

We all nodded at Drew and got up to leave. But Drew stopped us at the door with a question.

My heart dropped to my stomach at his words. It had slipped my mind for a few moments, but now that someone had asked, how was I supposed to answer? I wasn't a liar, and I didn't wish to attempt to be one.

I turned around carefully to look at my brother in the eye. That did not help my predicament.

"Quinn?" he repeated. "Did he call again?"

"I'll let you know if he does," I said as quickly as I dared without giving myself away.

Drew simply nodded, turning back to his work, so I pulled at Jess and Eli's shirt sleeves to make a hasty exit.

CHAPTER 32

Later, after we dropped Jess off and picked up Carter and Darby, the kids took it upon themselves to invite Eli over for supper. It definitely wasn't the first time, but it was the first time for him to come spend time with us now that we were an official item. Eli said yes to the invite.

Zindt was walking around my house when we pulled into Eli's driveway. He looked a little preoccupied, but he gave us a small smile and a wave as he headed back to his car.

Eli said he'd be over to help with supper after he washed up, so we headed into our house. A little while later, I was straining freshly cooked noodles in the sink when I saw Eli walking across the yard. His short dark hair looked a little wet, and he had on a dark blue, short-sleeve shirt and a pair of khaki shorts.

I looked down at my own attire. I still wore the clothes I'd had on all day. Suddenly, I felt self-conscious.

"Carter?" I asked about the time Eli knocked on the side door. "Will you let Eli in and y'all finish up the cooking?"

"Sure," Carter said, pulling chicken breasts out of the freezer.

"Thanks," I called over my shoulder, dashing around the corner and up the stairs to freshen up.

Thirty minutes later, I was showered, in fresh capri pants, and a purple sleeveless shirt with my hair pinned up, a few auburn curls spilling from a quick French twist. Eli had been around for every awkward phase of my childhood and on good days and bad days since. But I did want to look nice from him now.

I caught sight of the pictures of the cards on my way out of my bathroom. The top picture was of a white card with multicolored writing. The line there read:

"Of bold Sir Lancelot"

The back of the card said, "Who."

Most likely, that was fairly simple. Sir Lancelot was supposed to be a brave handsome knight. Ruby probably saw an older man just as ladies were rumored to have seen chivalrous knights—handsome and brave.

I sank into the chair at my desk, staring at the card.

"Poor girl," I murmured.

How sad it would be to be in love, only to be betrayed in the worst way imaginable. I didn't want to imagine what was going through the girl's head the moment he took her life away.

"Lord, help us," I prayed quietly as I started to get up. "Keep us safe."

I stiffened the moment I stood up at the shrill sound of my phone. I turned to see it on my desk where I'd put it as I went to shower.

How could I forget?

I took a deep breath.

"Yes," I said upon answering the phone.

"Congratulations, you passed," he said.

"Consider me thrilled."

He chuckled. "Well, if we haven't found our spunk."

"I don't—"

"Yes, dear, I know," he said.

My skin crawled when he referred to me as "dear."

"You don't have it," he said. "And if you do, you haven't found it. But it seems you and little Miss Beth have...communicated."

I didn't reply. I don't know how he knew that, but he wasn't too specific, so I wasn't going to fill him in.

"I am tired of waiting," he said. "So you better make it quick. Don't tell anyone I called."

"Look—"

"No." That one word was the harshest command I'd ever heard in my life. "Figure it out by this time tomorrow, or you most definitely won't be able to live with the consequences of your failure."

I didn't even have time to gasp at his threat because the phone clicked in my ear.

Tomorrow?

I didn't know what to do for a second. Consequences of my failure? What? I looked around frantically.

What did that mean, exactly?

"Quinn?"

I jumped, startled.

I whipped around toward the door to see Eli standing in the doorway.

"Eli," I mumbled, my mind swimming.

He cleared the short space between the doorway and me in one second. He looked down and saw my hand clutching the phone.

"He called," Eli said immediately. He gently pulled the phone from my grip and tossed it onto my bed. "Quinn, it's okay. I'm here. We'll call Drew and—"

"No—" I cried out, suddenly. "I can't. He, I can't, Eli. Please help me. I have to figure out where that necklace is by tomorrow night."

He looked worried.

"Quinn—" he began.

"No, Eli," I told him, quickly. "Don't try to get me to call my brother." My mind raced on to what exactly the man might be threatening. I had to figure this out quick. "We need to get the kids their supper and settled for the night. Then we need to look at these cards. Will you help me? Please?"

He pulled me to him suddenly without speaking. Peace washed over me, flooding my worried frantic mind. I buried my face in his chest, and he squeezed me kissing the top of my head.

"You know I will, Quinn," he assured me. "Anything you need, all you have to do is ask."

CHAPTER 33

After supper and dishes and getting Darby and Carter squared
away upstairs, I carried the pictures down to John's old office
and spread them out on his desk. Eli pulled up a chair to one
side while I sat in John's old desk chair and refreshed Eli about what
I had decided about the clues.

"Well, Drew checked Blalock's boat, and I'm sure Mr. Scott's by
now," Eli thought aloud. "We tore Jess's boat apart, and Drew and
his deputies have searched around here twice." He stopped a minute.
"Are you sure? It's on a boat?"

"The clue says, 'Where'," I told him. "The line says, 'Round
about the prow she wrote.' It has to be a boat."

We stared at the pictures, stumped. We couldn't search every
boat in town.

"She said she knew I could figure it out," I said, absently, my
eyes running over all the pictures one by one. "I have to, Eli. He's…
crazy. Like the guy in "Porphyria's Lover." He's already killed two
people. That we know of. He won't hesitate to—"

Eli grabbed my hand to stop the flow.

"Look at me, Quinn," he said, so I did. "You will. We will. It
will be okay."

I smiled, reassured by his confidence. Then I looked back to the
pictures.

"Will you hand me the book of poetry?" Eli asked a few
moments later.

I passed it to him while I read the lines in the pictures over and
over. I heard the pages flip but didn't look up.

"Quinn?" Eli asked after a few minutes of silence.

"Hmmm?" I mumbled.

"She wrote her name about the prow," he said.

I looked up. I knew that; I'd read the poem dozens of times over the years.

"Yes," I agreed.

"It's not on a boat," he said, flatly.

A few puzzle pieces slid together in my head.

"Her name," I whispered. "It's with her name."

"But which name?" Eli pointed out.

"No," I corrected. "Not Leigh's name. The Lady of Shalott, her name."

I jumped up grabbing Eli's arm. He stumbled around the desk to follow after me.

"How could I be so stupid?" I scolded myself as I dashed up the stairs with Eli close on my heels.

"What?" Eli asked, skidding to a stop just behind me, right inside my bedroom door.

"I need to kick myself," I told him as I stepped into a chair in front of my bookshelf to grab a small photo frame from the top of it.

The picture frame sat where it always had. "The Lady of Shalott" had been my favorite poem long before I ever met Leigh Taylor. John had found a small picture in an old book that depicted a woman sitting at a loom. It was in a book of poetry, and under the picture, in small type, it said, "THE LADY OF SHALOTT." John cut out the picture and put it in a small, pretty frame. Whoever it was that tossed my room days before never moved it. I think I surprised them, so they may not have had the opportunity to rummage through everything.

I took it over to my bed and turned it over. The back of the frame bulged a little.

I stopped.

"Eli," I said, laying the frame down on the bed, "will you go get me a plastic sandwich bag?"

He nodded and was gone while I headed to my bathroom to get a pair of tweezers.

I was back to the picture frame a few seconds before Eli.

"My fingerprints are already on the outside of the frame," I told him, my attention on opening the back of the frame. "Will you hold the bag open?"

He did so, but when I pulled the back off, it wasn't the necklace.

A folded sheet of paper popped out.

Eli and I exchanged a confused glance.

"More clues?" Eli guessed.

I shrugged.

"Gil said she was getting paranoid," I said. "He must've been right."

I grabbed one corner of the paper with the tweezers and used the plastic bag Eli had brought to cover my fingers so I could unfold it.

It was addressed to me again, and it was also in Leigh's neat square handwriting, just as the other letter and the note cards.

Quinn,

I'm sorry for all the subterfuge, but I had to be extremely careful and very sneaky. Gil thinks I'm paranoid, but he's just worried about me. ☺

Go to the upper stacks in the library at the school.

Call number 812. I knew no one would bother it until you or I could get back to it.

All I have that could point a finger straight at him is in that book!

Your Friend,
Leigh

"I wish you could have found this note first! We need to get this to Drew ASAP," Eli said after he read the paper over my shoulder.

I left the paper on the bed to get my phone, but I forgot that I'd left it in John's study.

"Be right back," I told him.

He nodded trying to fold the paper back up without touching it and get it into the plastic bag.

At the bottom of the stairs, I saw Deputy Zindt through the glass of the front door. He was walking up the front steps, still in plain clothes. His badge on the clip at his waist gleamed for a second in the glow from the porch light.

He was about to knock on the door when he noticed me already on my way to it. He smiled as I pulled the door open.

"Just checking in," he told me. "And a restroom break before y'all settle in for the night."

"Oh, sure," I said, stepping aside to let him in. "But y'all are probably about to be hopping again in a few minutes."

"Oh?" he asked, looking curious.

"Yes," I told him. "Eli and I found another note. I came down here to get my phone to call Drew."

"I'll call him," he told me. "Can you go get the note for me?"

"Yes," I said, heading for the stairs. I was so focused on calling my brother that I didn't even think about getting the cop who was sitting in my front yard.

Back upstairs, Eli was just heading out of my room after finally getting the letter folded up and tucked safely away in the plastic bag.

"Zindt's calling Drew," I told him. "Will you check on Carter and Darby while I take that down to him?"

"Sure," he said, handing over the bag and leaning in to kiss my cheek.

My heart fluttered for a second.

"Told you we'd figure it out," he said, happily.

We parted ways—he went to check on the kids, and I went back downstairs to Zindt.

"Yes, sir," Zindt said as I got to the bottom of the stairs. He tapped the touchscreen on his phone and slid the phone into his pocket.

I left Zindt for a minute to go retrieve my phone from John's study before I forgot. It was lying by the open book of poetry Eli had left on John's desk.

For some reason, a line caught my eye. In my room earlier, I had just been thinking about how poor Ruby had been suckered in by a handsome man. The particular line that caught my eye just then described Lancelot's hair. I don't know why it hadn't occurred to me before, but I guess it was because this particular hint never made it into any of Leigh's clues.

I must have stared at the line longer than I thought because I jumped at a touch on my elbow. But Zindt didn't look particularly startled when I yelped.

"Sorry," I apologized, shoving my phone into my pocket. "You just startled me. What did Drew say?"

"I'm going to meet him at the school," Zindt said.

"Good, I'll go with you," I said, quickly, before he could elaborate.

"No, ma'am," he said, firmly. "The sheriff said for you to stay here."

"Why?" I snapped with a little bit more force than I had intended. "Sorry. I mean, why can't I go? Leigh involved me in all of this, and obviously the cops are there. It's safe."

"Ms. Kelley—" he started, but I cut him off.

"If you don't take me with you, I will just follow you." I crossed my arms over my chest and stared him down. They were all right to assume I was extremely hardheaded no matter if I argued just the opposite with every one about it.

"Quinn, the sheriff—" he started again.

"My big brother is just going to have to get over it," I cut him off again. "I want to help these poor ladies whose lives were stolen from them by a psycho who used his looks and charm to reel in a teenager and then proceeded to poison her sister when she got too close to the truth. They deserve some sort of justice, and I plan to be the person to do that for them. In the very least, I want to actively help get rid of this monster. No one deserves that harsh of a betrayal, especially a teenage girl who should have had her whole life ahead of her. Leigh didn't deserve her tragic end either."

He was quiet for a moment. If he was truly taken by surprise at my words in any way, he didn't show it. He just seemed to contemplate me determining if I would really follow him like I said I would or not.

Apparently, I was convincing.

"Okay," he conceded with a sigh. "I guess it might be worse if you showed up after me. But I think the sheriff is going to flip his lid."

I couldn't help but smile.

"Don't worry," I assured him. "I can talk him down."

I darted around him calling for Eli, who appeared suddenly from the kitchen. He had a few choice words about my need to go with Zindt, but I countered back.

"We're wasting time," I told him. "Obviously, the kids will be fine with you here, and I will be OK because I will be surrounded by sheriff's deputies."

"That is *not* the point, Quinn," Eli said, sternly.

"Eli, please," I tried a little softer tone. "I need to go. She left it for me to find."

He didn't get any happier with my statement, but at least he seemed to realize what it meant to me. He already knew, he was just worried about me.

I was about to say something else, but the thought was quickly gone when Eli grasped both sides of my face and pulled me to him, planting a solid kiss on my lips. Our first real kiss.

I gasped, not expecting that to be his reaction, especially not in front of Zindt. But for certain, I kissed him back.

"Be careful," he whispered against my lips when he pulled back a hair. "I don't want you to get hurt, you hard-headed thing. I love you."

Even in the midst of all that was going on, I couldn't help but smile.

"And I love you," I assured him.

Zindt cleared his throat, as I am sure he was feeling pretty awkward right then. So Zindt and I left with my head still swimming with too many awesome and terrible thoughts all swirling around too close together.

CHAPTER 34

The drive back into town and to the school only took about fifteen minutes. But it was a quiet ride. Zindt usually talked to me when the opportunity arose, but he was concentrating on the drive and, I'm sure, the job ahead of him. I was concentrating on the line of that poem, staring out the window.

The line about Lancelot's hair. It had to confirm the killer.

At least it did to my mind, anyway.

Mr. Scott was an adult in Ruby's life. He had access to her. While he was the standoffish type who kept his personal life to himself, he was a very handsome man. I could completely understand Ruby falling for his quiet, good looks.

And he had coal black curls, just like Sir Lancelot in the poem.

We were already looking toward him, anyway. This had to prove it!

I jumped again when Zindt touched my elbow. He had turned off the vehicle because we were parked in front of the school.

"Sorry," I apologized again. "Just lost in thought over this."

"Understandable," he said quietly with a nod of his head.

"Ummm, where's Drew?" I asked, scanning the dim parking lot. It was usually well-lit, but a few of the lights weren't working near where we were parked.

Zindt checked his watch.

"He'll be here shortly," Zindt confirmed. "He was out on a call when I talked to him."

I nodded. If he was on a call, then it could possibly take him a bit to untangle himself from that situation before he could head out to meet us.

"I have my key to the front door," I offered. "We can go ahead. I'll show you the stacks. I'll let you take care of it. I promise I won't touch anything."

He cracked half a smile for just a second.

"That works," he agreed. "The sheriff said to keep you with me and he'd be here as soon as he could. We can go ahead."

My heart jumped a little knowing I was going to the last piece of the puzzle. In my mind, I knew the truth, but I wanted to see it, for sure, from whatever Leigh had hidden in the stacks.

I unlocked the front door to the school and walked on through with Zindt close behind me. I'd only taken a few steps into the hall before I thought it'd probably be better if the guy with the gun went first. I could point out exactly where to go.

I turned on my heel just in time to see a shadowy figure loom up behind Zindt.

The scream caught in my throat, but Zindt caught the shock on my face. He tried to whip around to face the figure but only made half a turn before getting smacked in the side of the face with a fire extinguisher.

He dropped like a stone, and I gasped.

I stumbled backward a few steps before the figure stepped over Zindt's crumpled form, coming into the dimly lighted area of the hall under the security lights.

His coal black hair actually shone brightly in the light.

Somehow, my voice found me again.

"Mr. Scott," I eeked out.

"Quinn," he said quietly, reaching out a hand to me.

That slight movement was like a jolt of lightning to my skin.

I didn't hesitate.

I jerked around and ran off into the darkness as Mr. Scott called after me.

CHAPTER 35

For a few moments, my brain buzzed, and all I could do was run headlong through the darkened hallway. If I hadn't known the place so well, just the eerie stillness and nighttime quiet of the school probably would have unnerved me right there. But I held onto my presence of mind as best as I could.

The sound of my name echoing in the dark halls jolted my heart again—I had to hide!

"No!" I said aloud, screeching to a halt, almost tripping over my own feet. "I have to get that evidence."

So far, only Eli, Zindt, Drew, and I knew where the thing was, and I needed to get it. I couldn't leave it.

I took off again, making sure my steps were quieter now, heading toward the janitor's closet that would lead to the stacks. I figured it was less conspicuous than the front doors to the library.

My heart almost dropped at the thought that the door might be locked, but a sigh escaped me as the door clicked open. I hurried in and shut the door noiselessly behind me.

In a matter of seconds, I was through the back door at the back of the closet and up the old stairs. It was only a matter of a few more moments, and I found the book Leigh had indicated. I started to grab it but cringed. I didn't want to contaminate any evidence.

Then the proverbial light bulb clicked on inside my head— there were gloves in the janitor's closet.

I took a quick scan over the railing down into the library, and from what I could see from the strategically placed security lighting, there was no sign of Mr. Scott. Or Zindt for that matter.

Silently, I prayed Zindt was okay—and that he would help me out—as I quietly made my way to go get the gloves from the janitor's closet. Next to the box of gloves, I saw a box of plastic bags, so I grabbed one of those, too. Back up the stairs, I glanced around the upper stacks, but I didn't see any movement.

My heart had calmed down for a few moments when I was getting the gloves. I had given myself something to concentrate on. But back at the top of the stairs, staring out into the quiet of the semidarkness, my heart sped up again.

I almost couldn't make myself go through the door, but I knew I had to retrieve what Leigh had left. It felt as if all my hairs were standing on end, and I just knew I was going to get knocked in the head, but I made myself leave the doorway at the top of the stairs and go back to the book Leigh had indicated.

It was in the Literature section—800s call numbers. 812 to be exact.

Inside a book of O. Henry short stories.

My hand stopped again before I touched the book. Earlier, I had just located the call number 812. I hadn't paid attention to the title—I could barely see the faded title in the dim lighting. But I had had it in the back of my mind that it would be in a book of poetry.

But, O. Henry?

Everything Leigh had done had been to clue me in to who had really murdered her sister. This was no different; I was sure of that.

The wheels in my head started turning.

O. Henry stories all have a twist. They have some sort of irony that hits you in the face near the end of the story. You think you know how the story is going to turn out, then wham!

The end is not what you expect!

"The end is not what I expect," I whispered to myself.

My heart sank completely.

"Oh crap," I mumbled.

Hurriedly, I scrambled to get the book off the shelf. Just about the second I opened the book, a click echoed in the library.

I whipped around, but the door to the back stairs of the janitor's closet was closed, and I didn't see anyone. Unfortunately, though, in my whip around to check the door, I dropped the book.

It landed with only a soft thud, but if I could hear the click of the door echo, then whoever opened a door in there could hear that book drop.

And I couldn't wait for them to find me.

A sealed envelope was sticking out of the book, so I grabbed it up in my still-gloved hand and placed it in the plastic bag as I made a mad dash for the door to the back stairs. As the door was swinging closed behind me, I heard footfalls coming from inside the library.

I dashed down the stairs and into the janitor's closet, hoping against hope that I could get out of there before Scott caught up with me—if that was who was still pursuing me.

And if O. Henry was a clue for me to be ready for a twist, then who really was the killer?

CHAPTER 36

I thought I'd had it all figured out, but I had to be missing something. Leigh wouldn't have chosen an O. Henry book as a hiding spot for no reason.

But as I hurried as quietly as I could down the darkened hallway, I could hear my brother in the back of my head, telling me this wasn't my job to figure out. And my next thought was just where in the world was he anyway? Zindt called him from my house, and even if Drew had been out on a call, he would have made sure that he squared that away with the deputies and then got to the school as quickly as possible.

Maybe he was here and had a run-in with Scott, too. And if there was a twist, and the killer wasn't who I thought it was—Scott—then why did he smack Zindt in the head?

I rounded a corner of the hall, finally realizing I was headed back to the front door. I guess, subconsciously, I was trying to get out of the building and my foot slipped suddenly.

I was just able to regain my balance before I toppled completely over, only to look down and see my foot was in a smudge of dark on the tiled floor.

"Blood," I breathed out.

This was where Zindt had fallen, and there was a fairly large amount of blood on the floor. My foot had slipped in it.

But where was Zindt?

I scanned the hallway, finally seeing a smeared trail leading to the auditorium doors.

Should I check on him? I thought, hesitating in the hall. *Or should I try to get Drew?*

In the next second, the decision was made for me.

"Quinn!"

The sound of my name split the silence in the hallway. My head jerked in the direction of the sound, the way I had just came from, and I saw Scott fly around the corner.

The doors to the auditorium were closer to me than the front doors, so I made a mad dash for the auditorium.

It was almost like diving headfirst into a dark lake. There were no security lights on in the auditorium, except behind some curtains on the stage, so I ran, hoping my eyes would adjust to the dimmer lighting before I fell over something.

I made it to a darker spot up near the stage when I heard the door fling open with a bang. I automatically dropped to the floor feeling the need to hide.

"Quinn!" Mr. Scott called out. "Will you stop running and listen to me?"

My heart kicked into overdrive then. I still didn't know enough to trust him while I was alone, so I quietly kept moving on the floor while I could hear that he was at the back of the auditorium.

"Quinn!" he called out again.

About the same time, my foot hit a wall. But my eyes had adjusted enough, and I had gotten closer to some lighting that I could see I was at the side stairs to the stage.

If I could get to the office at the back of the stage, there was a phone in there. I could call Drew.

Scott was still moving around back there, probably trying to see if I was hiding in the rows of seats. So I took advantage of the stage curtain and scrambled up the few stairs to the stage, careful to stay in the shadows. It was then that I luckily remembered I had slipped in Zindt's blood out in the hall, so I quickly slipped off my sneakers and quietly dropped them in a dark corner. I couldn't risk leaving a bloody-footprint trail right to me!

I stayed behind the various curtains that were strategically layered on the stage. A prop or two helped me hide my maneuvering as well. It only took a few moments, and I was in the director's office.

I thanked the Lord right then that Ms. Hartnett, the drama teacher, was rather messy. I crouched down next to the desk in case Scott made it on stage so that he wouldn't spot me easily. But from my crouched position, it was hard to locate the phone in the mass of scripts, costumes, and coffee cups that covered the desk.

Finally, my hand grasped the familiar object, and I took the receiver off the cradle. Again, I silently thanked the good Lord; I could dial the phone without looking, and I knew Drew's number by heart.

He picked up on the second ring. Before he could finish, "Hello," I was snapping at him.

"Drew, where the heck are you?" I griped in a whisper. "Why aren't you at the school yet?"

"School?" he asked, his voice full of surprise. "Quinn? Is that you?"

"Of course, it's me!" I snapped a little louder than I had intended, so I crouched down even farther, scared that I had revealed myself to Scott.

"What are you—" he began, but I cut him off again.

"Drew, stop asking questions and get your behind over here, now!" I whispered with all the force I could muster and as loud as I dared. "You should have been here by now, anyway."

"What?" he snapped back. "Why? Why are you even there? Why aren't you at home?"

"Home?" I exclaimed. "We're at the school, and now Scott is after me, and Zindt has disappeared, and he was out cold and bleeding the last time I saw him, and..."

"Scott? Zindt?" he interrupted. "I have an officer down?"

There was a muffled sound, then words I couldn't make out, and then he was speaking to me again.

"Quinn, are you okay? What's going on? Why is Scott after you?"

He spat the questions in rapid succession, but I only really caught on to the last one.

"Drew! Dang it!" I snapped again. "You know what's going on! Zindt called you! So why aren't you here already?"

There was a pause on the other end of the line that was just long enough and just silent enough to make the light switch go on in my head even before my brother spoke the words I knew he was about to say.

"Quinn," he said, quietly and evenly. "Zindt never called me."

CHAPTER 37

My heart sank with the realization. Why hadn't it hit me like a ton of bricks after I found the papers in the O. Henry book and then couldn't find Zindt?!

"Lord, help me," I whispered to myself. Then, into the phone, "The school, now, Drew!"

Suddenly, I heard Scott again, so I put the receiver down on the phone.

"Quinn!" he called out, but I wasn't about to answer him.

He may not have killed Ruby, but something still wasn't right with him. He had clocked Zindt with a fire extinguisher, and then he'd asked me to "let him explain."

Explain what, though?

And I couldn't just sit where I was. I had to move!

And Drew needed the envelope I'd found. If Zindt caught me with it, it may not make it back to Drew.

I glanced around the side of the desk and could see Scott on the stage, looking in a prop closet. But there was no sign of Zindt, which was scarier.

My mind tried to drift to him and Ruby, but I tried to stay focused on the present situation. So I glanced around the dim cluttered office.

If I hid it in this mess, we would never find it again!

But as I looked around, I saw that one of the old, heavy-as-lead filing cabinets had just a smidgen of clearance between it and the wall. So I chanced another look around the desk out the door to make sure neither Scott nor Zindt knew where I was. I didn't see either one at that point, so I crawled over to the filing cabinet and slid the envelope in between the cabinet and the wall. If either one of them came in there looking for it, they weren't likely to find it right away—they would probably dig through the mass of papers first, and that cabinet was too heavy to just be tossing around.

Fairly certain it was safe for a time, I made my way over to the door, crouching low and keeping quiet. I stopped in the shadow by the door frame just in time to see Scott walk right past the door.

My heart leapt into my throat for a second, but I had to take my chance. He had just about covered all the places I might have hidden on the stage; he was bound to come in the office at any moment.

So I took a deep breath and dashed out the door, heading for the edge of the stage. It was only about a three and a half foot drop at the edge. I could jump down and jet for the door.

The sheriff's office wasn't that far away. Drew should be here fast. I just needed to keep away from them a few more minutes.

And I almost made it.

At the edge of the stage, I took a leap to jump down to the auditorium floor, and I was suspended in air for a moment.

Right before I felt a backward jerk on my arms and landed on my rear end on the stage with a thud. Through my wincing, I looked up to see a bloody Jay Zindt looming over me.

CHAPTER 38

I gasped and tried to scramble backward, but I hit the couch that was a prop on stage. Then, suddenly, Mr. Scott was standing off to my right, only a few feet away from Zindt. I couldn't help but look back and forth between the two of them. Standing that close, the resemblance couldn't be denied.

"You're brothers?" I half-asked, half-declared.

"Yes," Mr. Scott said. "That's part of what I was trying to explain, Quinn. He's my half-brother. We have different fathers."

"Oh, shut up, Reeve!" Zindt snapped. "She doesn't need our family history."

"You need to calm down, Jay," Mr. Scott said to his brother, taking half a step toward him. "This doesn't have to be like Ruby."

My heart stopped for a second.

Oh, my Lord! I thought. What was it "like" with Ruby? Were they both in on it?

I should have kept my mouth shut, but my mind had failed to function properly being in a room with a murderer, possibly two murderers.

"Why did you kill that poor girl?" I snapped with more force than I had intended.

Mr. Scott was the only one to look shocked. His head whipped toward me with a look of surprise and disgust on his face.

"I didn't," he insisted. "I—"

"Shut up, Reeve," Zindt snapped, shoving his brother, hard. Mr. Scott stumbled back a step.

I scrambled to my feet in the brief second of their distraction, but Zindt whipped around and latched onto my arm. His hand was an iron grip!

"Jay, stop!" Mr. Scott tried to reason with his brother. "Not a—"

"Shut up!" Zindt virtually growled this time, making my skin crawl as I pulled against his grip.

He literally sounded evil! He was oozing it now. It seemed as if he was an entirely different person than the man I had known for the last few years.

Panic set in, and I tried to squirm out of his grip, punching at his chest with my free hand.

"You monster! Let go!" I yelled at him.

"Monster!" he growled back, gripping me by both arms and jerking me so close that we were nearly nose to nose.

"Monster!" he growled again. "How am I the monster?"

"Jay!"

"Because you killed Ruby!" I snapped and pushed against him, scared, unable to think or hold my tongue or my temper. "And you killed Leigh!"

Zindt growled in rage and raised one hand to slap me, but Mr. Scott yanked me from Zindt's grip and stepped in between us.

"I'm not a monster!" Zindt yelled.

"Jay!" Mr. Scott yelled in his brother's face this time. "Stop this!"

"It doesn't matter what you say," I cried out around Smith's shoulder at his brother. "They're dead, and you killed them!"

"Get out of my way," Zindt said through gritted teeth, pulling his gun. "There's no other way now. Ruby and Leigh are gone, like she said. At this point, one more won't matter...and I'm not going to jail."

"But..." Scott began, only to be cut off by the best sound I had heard in a long time—my brother's voice.

"Drop your gun, Zindt," my brother said firmly.

I peeked around Scott and Zindt to see Drew coming down the center aisle of the auditorium as Alvarez flipped on some of the overhead lights. Drew's gun was trained on Zindt.

"I don't think so, sheriff," Zindt answered, slowly turning around to face my brother.

Scott took the opportunity of Zindt's diverted attention to quietly edge us away from his brother. He kept himself between me and Zindt as we slowly backed a few feet away.

"You don't have a choice, Zindt," Drew assured him as he continued down the center aisle, one steady step at a time.

Scott gently pushed us back another step. We weren't making a sound, but Zindt must have caught the slight movement out of the corner of his eye.

My heart jumped in my throat as the world slipped into slow motion. I could see Zindt's head jerk toward us. I could hear my brother shout Zindt's name, but his voice sounded deeper and far away. I could see Scott wheeling around to face me, putting himself solidly between his brother and me.

I saw the glint of the gun as Zindt raised his hand.

I didn't have time to scream. The world suddenly sped up as Scott threw himself against me, and we toppled to the ground.

The shot echoed through the auditorium right before I lost my breath from being knocked to the ground on my back.

Scott saved me!

I gasped for breath, trying to gain my bearings. Scott whipped his head around, still half shielding me.

Even in my gasping to get air back in my lungs, I could hear Scott cry out when he saw his brother.

Zindt lay on his stomach in a pool of blood, his face toward us and his wide-open eyes lifeless.

CHAPTER 39

As it turned out, the last clue Leigh left was a key to yet another safety deposit box in a bank forty miles away from Sutter. In the safety deposit box were the missing files from Leigh's stack of files, a thumb drive, and a DVD.

Of course, this wasn't made public knowledge, but I nagged my brother into divulging the info. I couldn't go another day without knowing just what happened to Ruby and what all Mr. Scott knew and what Leigh had on that thumb drive and DVD.

When Drew came over to give me the details, though, I'm not so sure he expected an audience. I had sent Carter and Darby with my mom for supper and assembled Eli, Bess, and Jess at the kitchen table around pizza, salad, and sweet tea.

My brother stopped short after closing the front door.

"Quinn—" he began.

"Oh, save it," I cut him off and then smiled. "We have supper. Besides, we're all best friends. What we know, they know and vice versa, so save yourself the time and just sit down."

He sighed as he dropped down into a chair. If he didn't tell them, I would. It wouldn't go any farther than that, but we all worked with Leigh and cared for her—we needed to know.

"Well, according to Scott, he only recently found out about Ruby," Drew began as he grabbed for a glass of tea and then took a sip from the tall glass.

Bess got up to start dishing out pizza on paper plates and filling everyone's bowls with salad.

"Do you believe him?" I asked.

"I didn't know what to believe at first," Drew conceded. "But then we figured out about the safety deposit box. Somehow Leigh had managed to bug Zindt's house, complete with cameras, without him knowing, and everything she gathered was on the thumb drive and the DVD."

"And it assured you that Scott was telling the truth?" Jess asked. "I mean, that he only knew about Ruby recently."

Drew nodded. "Yes. It seems Zindt had too much to drink one night and spilled the beans to his brother. According to Scott, Zindt was always hotheaded, and Zindt never stayed in one place very long. He's probably been here longer than he's been anywhere else. Well, Scott and Zindt always stayed near each other, getting jobs and homes never too far from the other. Sometimes, they even lived together. Scott did what he could to keep his brother under control, even covering up for him when Zindt would fly off the handle."

"Then how'd Zindt get a job with you?" Eli asked, curious. "I know you checked him out."

"I did," Drew agreed. "But apparently, some references were faked, and I've never heard of any complaints from the law enforcement in other areas that we've worked with."

"That's scary," Bess piped up. "Danger was right under our noses, and no one knew."

Drew nodded in agreement, a pained look crossing his face.

"And Ruby?" I asked. "Was there anything in that evidence that explained what happened to her?"

Drew sighed and looked out the front window into the quiet evening. I knew it hurt him even more when a case involved the young and innocent, and poor Ruby seemed to have been a young woman whose innocence was wiled away from her by an older man.

He looked back to us.

"It was an accident," Drew said flatly.

"What?" we all gasped in unison.

"An accident?" I cried. "But..."

"I don't believe Zindt had any reason to lie because he didn't know he was being recorded," Drew explained when I was too shocked to know what to even ask. "After listening to and watching everything in the safety deposit box, the short version is that he lost his temper with Ruby one day, and it scared her. So when she saw him again, she decided to break it off with him. Naturally, he was upset, and they argued.

"There was a secluded, old iron bridge where they used to meet, and that's where they were that day. She turned to leave, she was upset too, and he grabbed her backpack which caused her to stumble. The bridge was old and in disrepair. She fell on a protruding piece of iron, and it impaled her."

Bess and I gasped involuntarily at the news. Bess recovered enough to ask, "But why didn't he just tell the police?"

"He was the police," Drew said. "Twenty-two years old and on his first job as a city policeman. She was underage, so the whole mix was illegal, anyway."

"But they never found her," Eli stated, quietly.

Drew shook his head. "Zindt admitted to Scott he buried her but didn't say where."

For a few minutes, no one knew what to say. The whole situation was just too tragic. Two deaths, so many lives affected, one body never found, all over an accident!

I fully believed that Zindt had murdered Ruby. From all the clues in the poems, I thought for sure that he had killed Ruby, and then killed Leigh when she got too close, and somehow that a senseless accident had caused all of this hurt even worse.

"What will happen to Scott?" Jess broke the silence a few moments later.

Drew shrugged. "That'll be up to the district attorney. The info that Leigh gathered through the bug and the cameras in Zindt's home are inadmissible in court, but Scott seems to be telling us everything he knows. He only knew about Ruby for a short time, but he did know Zindt's propensity to lose his temper. And...he saved my little sister."

His last statement grabbed my attention from my frozen stupor. I was still contemplating the sadness of it all.

"That's true," I agreed. "He did."

"He'll never work in a school again," Drew sighed. "But a judge and jury will have to decide his fate."

EPILOGUE

Late in May, just a few days prior to graduation, I sat on my front porch grading a stack of final exams. The day was a beautiful one, and with the end of school so close, I was chomping at the bit for summertime.

The nearly two months since Leigh's death had flown by fast and furious. There was never a day where Leigh or Ruby didn't cross our minds in some way, but time moved on, and we had to move with it.

I sighed and smiled, remembering my sweet friend as I checked off an answer on a paper. The student had written "The Lady of Shalott" in the blank on the paper. That poem, my favorite poem of all, would always be a tie to my friend and, by extension, her little sister, whom I never had a chance to meet. Most of the clues that ended up leading us to Leigh and Ruby's killer had been embedded in that poem. It would always have a special meaning to me.

A breeze kicked up, ruffling some of the stack of papers in front of me, pulling me from my thoughts.

"Still grading?" a familiar voice said as I straightened the papers.

I smiled, looking up to see Eli. For some reason, it still felt strange that my heart flip-flopped whenever I saw him.

Why had it taken me so long to realize I loved him? I thought.

"Yep," I said, smiling up at him. "I'm helping out Leigh's substitute to get everything graded."

"Ah, I see," he nodded.

Jess had been promoted temporarily when Mr. Scott was arrested. The school board voted him in, officially, as the new principal of Sutter High School, the month after Leigh died. He had quickly hired a permanent sub to fill in for Leigh's position and appointed Bess and I her mentors and helpers.

There would be several changes at work before school picked up again in August. But at that moment, I just wanted to be through with the end of the school year and rest for a bit.

"How about you take a break and go for a walk with me?" Eli asked, flashing me his best smile.

I looked at my stack of papers again. I had made a considerable dent in it, so I figured a break wouldn't hurt.

Plus, it was getting harder and harder to resist that smile.

As quickly as I could, I gathered the papers into my school bag and set it inside the house and then shut the door and headed off down the steps with Eli. We walked, hand in hand, down the road, past his house. After only a few yards past Eli's house, the mail truck came bobbing along. The driver slowed down and eased around us, waving as he drove by.

"New mail man?" Eli questioned as we both waved back. "What happened to Lou?"

"Retired," I answered. "I talked to Cora Combs at the post office yesterday. That's the new guy, Devon McHugh."

"McHugh?" Eli repeated. "Hmmm. Never heard of him."

"Me neither," I said with a shrug.

We went on about our walk, the new mail man forgotten as we neared the stand of trees near Mr. Pressman's pond about a half a mile away from our houses. It was our favorite spot to sit and enjoy a beautiful day.

I should have known something was up when we got closer to the stand of trees and there was already a blanket spread out with a picnic basket sitting on it. But it took me *years* to realize that I loved Eli and he loved me, so, obviously, I'm pretty dense with the romance stuff.

All I clicked to was a picnic, so all I said was, "Oh look! A picnic!"

Eli just laughed and gestured for me to sit down. As I did, he unpacked the picnic basket, a grin spread across his face.

"What in the world are you grinning about?" I asked, curious.

"You," he said, finally settling down on the blanket next to me.

I blushed in response.

"Well, Mr. Bloom," I drawled out, "I feel the same way about you."

"I'm glad we're on the same page." He leaned in for a kiss, making my heart flutter. I silently hoped his kisses would always do that to me.

When he pulled away, my face was still flushed, and the afternoon seemed warmer than it had before.

Eli turned to the array of food on the blanket to grab a bottle of water and passed it on to me. I opened it, still flushed, and took a sip.

I was replacing the lid when it looked like something moved in my water.

"Eli!" I gasped. "There's something in here!"

He chuckled. "I know."

I was taken aback. Why would he let me drink water that had something floating in it? "What?"

I looked at the bottle, shaking it a little. I was about to protest again when the sunlight caught the water bottle just right, and sparkled brightly.

I gasped, words caught in my throat.

He was quiet for a moment before he spoke.

"Quinn," he said quietly, the grin gone, a soft, sweet smile in its place. "Are you that surprised?"

I searched for words that wouldn't come. Tears stung at the corners of my eyes.

Eli wanted to marry me!

His smile faded a little as I still sat there motionless, unable to speak.

"I already talked to Carter and Darby and your parents," he explained. "I even talked to your brother, while he was doing target practice, I might add."

He chuckled, a little nervously. Talking to Drew while he was heavily armed took guts, that was for sure.

"What...what did they all say?" I asked, barely above a whisper.

Eli relaxed again, his smile regaining its sweetness and worry retreating from his face.

"They say yes," he reported. "Your brother actually said, 'It's about dang time, Bloom!'"

I could feel the corners of my mouth soften into a small smile.

I loved Eli so much. Of course, I wanted to marry him. But for some reason, I couldn't get my own answer out.

Then I heard him. As plain as the sun that was shining in the sky that day, I heard him.

John Kelley, the only other man I had ever loved, said, "Be happy."

I spun around. I could have sworn he was standing right there!

After a few moments, Eli broke my silence.

"Quinn?"

I turned to see him looking around as I had been. Then he looked back to me.

"Yes," I said.

"Yes?" he repeated.

"Yes!" I cried this time, lunging forward and tackling him in a hug that knocked us both over.

He hugged me back, showering my face with kisses, repeating, I love you, over and over.

"Of course, it's yes," I told him, when I could get a word in between kisses. "There is no other answer."

He grinned and held my face in his hands.

"I don't want to wait to marry you," he said. "Let's get married this summer!"

I didn't want to wait to be his wife any more than he wanted to wait to be my husband.

"Well," I said with a grin, "there goes the restful summer I had in mind."

Eli chuckled at that response, and we spent the rest of the afternoon enjoying the sunshine, the food, and the expectation of our upcoming wedding.

ABOUT THE AUTHOR

April Drake loves to read and write and has dreamed of publishing her own stories since she was twelve years old. April earned her Bachelor's Degree in History from Lamar University in 2002, and she has been teaching History and English to students in a small town high school for the last seventeen years. She is a lifelong resident of Southeast Texas and hopes to continue to create stories set in her beloved home state.